One of the best ways to sho
missions is to expose him oi
sionaries. *The Man in the Green Jeep* is just that kind of story!
This book will help young minds to see the importance of taking the Gospel of Jesus Christ to cultures around the world.
—Reese Kauffman, President
    Child Evangelism Fellowship

The Man in the Green Jeep is an exciting story. It made me
think about people who need help. It was fun to read this
book, especially because the little boy was the same age as I
am. I liked all the adventures. This story will help people to
think about other people around the world.
—Tate Waechter, 11-year-old reader

Children will be intrigued by the life of Chico and his friends.
This fun read captures the attention and gives insight into the
way Christ can be made known by using means such as a
green Jeep, rabbits, and farming techniques. Adults and children alike will be inspired by the faithfulness and creativity of
those who will go to any length to help others enter into a personal relationship with Jesus Christ.
—Carolyn Porterfield, Executive Director-Treasurer
    Woman's Missionary Union of Texas

A wonderful book about the adventures of Chico and his fami-
ly. Readers discover the greatest adventure of all—knowing
God and being on mission with Him
—Keith Mack, Children and Youth Mission
    and Ministry Director
    Texas Baptist Men

This is a great missions story for children and adults! The story, told through the eyes of a child, helps people understand the way of life for many around the world and see the challenges they face. *The Man in the Green Jeep* demonstrates how the Gospel message changes families and communities.

—JuLee Davis
   Association of Christian Schools International Missions
   Education Coordinator

An exciting and captivating glance into children's lives and culture in a small mountain town in Honduras. Children will readily identify with Chico and his friends—Rafael, José, Marvin, and the "bully-turned-nice" Calvin—and their daily experiences. The work and ministry of "the man in the green Jeep" and his associates are introduced in exciting ways and give a challenging view of innovative missions.
—William E. (Bill) Young, Retired Manager
   Discipleship and Family Ministry Preschool and Children's
       Division
   LifeWay Christian Resources

The Man
IN THE
Green Jeep

VIOLA PALMER

☩HANNIBAL BOOKS
www.hannibalbooks.com

Printed in the United States of America
by Versa Press, Inc.
Cover design by Greg Crull
Study guide by Pam Day

Library of Congress Control Number: 2005923908
ISBN 0-929292-61-8

Hannibal Books
P.O. Box 461592
Garland, Texas 75046
1-800-747-0738
www.hannibalbooks.com

Dedicated to:

the memory of dear missionary friends,

Larry and Jean Elliott,

who were tragically killed in March, 2004,
while serving the Lord in Iraq.

I know they look down and smile
at what God is doing all across Honduras
because of their faithful service there.
"Hermano Larry" spent many days
ministering to the people of the Reitoca area,
alongside
my dear husband,
Jim—"The Man in the Green Jeep."

Contents

Chapter One
The Storm   11

Chapter Two
Aunt Sara's   25

Chapter Three
Help Arrives   33

Chapter Four
The Well   47

Chapter Five
The Fight   59

Chapter Six
The Wedding   73

Chapter Seven
Rosa's Trees   85

Chapter Eight
The Paved Road   95

Chapter Nine
Mama Gets Sick   111

Chapter Ten
The Rabbit Gift   121

Appendix
Study Guide for *The Man in the Green Jeep*   129

ONE

The Storm

*

The roaring wind slapped at the tin roof as the rain pelted down. In the black dark of the night, Chico could not see his hand in front of his face. Only the flash of lightning allowed Chico to see his papa looking out the window.

The booming thunder caused him to jump. Chico got up from his moist, straw mat on the dirt floor and crept to the window to look out.

In the next crack of lighting, Chico viewed nothing but muddy water for as far as he could see.

"Will it ever stop?" whispered Chico to his papa.

"Go back to your bed, Francisco," replied Papa gruffly, "before you wake your brothers and sisters."

Chico wanted to stay at the window, but he didn't want to wake the rest of his family, nor did he want to irritate his papa right now. Chico did that enough in the daytime. Papa had used Chico's full name, not his nickname, so he knew Papa was not happy. Chico tiptoed back to his mat.

Rosa, Chico's big sister whispered, "What do you see out there?" "Water is everywhere," whispered back Chico. "Looks like rain has fallen for three days and nights."

"Hmm," yawned Rosa, as she turned over and went back to sleep.

Chico lay on his side and worried about the rain. *What if the water washes away the house?* He turned over to his other side. *What will happen if the rain washes away the school building?* He turned to lie on his back. *If the rain continues, can I swim to the big tree and climb up its branches?*

Turning over again he thought, *Why can't I just quit thinking and go back to sleep like Rosa did?* Chico shivered, *Do I feel cold because I'm sleeping on this damp dirt, or am I shivering from fright?* Chico didn't want to admit that he was scared. He turned over again. *Maybe someday our family could be rich and have beds up off the ground.* He turned over again. *Quit thinking and go to sleep,* he commanded himself. He finally dozed off.

A bright light woke Chico. He jumped to his feet. Rapidly he took a few quick steps to the window. Sunshine! Wonderful sunshine! Their house had not been swept away by the water. The sunlight shimmered off the water on the leaves. Brown water ran in a muddy trench in front of the house.

Smiling at the sunlight he turned around and glanced at his brothers and sisters still dreaming as they lay on their straw mats on the damp, dirt floor.

Rosa, his older sister, was lying on the floor with Lupe, their baby brother, in the crook of her arm. Rosa usually got up earlier than Chico did to help their mother fix breakfast. His little brother, Abel, was snuggled up to Rosa's backside. His little sister, Nanci, lay at an odd angle, with the damp sheet twisted around her leg.

Normally Chico could hear birds singing, donkeys braying, and roosters crowing. He shivered. The quiet seemed to say that things were not right.

12

Chico moved to the kitchen door and watched as Mama put water in a pot over the fire.

"Where is Papa?" Chico whispered. He did not want to wake his brothers and sisters.

"He's gone to the fields to see what damage the wind and rain did to the corn," replied Mama as she added coffee to the water. "Why don't you run down there with him?"

"All right," shrugged Chico. He wanted to get outside in the sunshine. Three days inside this house was enough! He did not want to bother his papa. Staying inside the house for three days in the driving rain with his father, who was frustrated about being inside, had been rough. Chico couldn't even remember what he had done to upset him. Papa got displeased so easy that Chico had trouble keeping Papa happy with him.

"Don't say or do anything to upset him," warned Mama.

"Okay, I'll be good," sighed Chico.

The squish, squish of the mud oozed between his toes. The sunshine began to warm his body. Soon the warm sun would dry up the mud.

As Chico walked toward the fields, he remembered working in the corn field last week before the rain started. He had pulled weeds until his back ached. He had begged his papa to let him quit. But he could not quit until his job was done. The corn had been tall with little ears just waiting to grow big enough to be picked in a few weeks. This would make tortillas—the family's main food. Tortillas were the only bread Chico ever had known.

Chico walked over the hills toward his papa's fields. Half an hour later he reached the edge of the corn field. He opened his eyes wide. It looked all wrong. *Where is the corn? What happened?* Lying on the ground were the green stalks. The winds had taken the tall, straight stalks of corn and bent them into the ground. Looking out over the sop-

13

ping wet field, Chico saw his father trying to stand the flattened corn back up. But the corn wouldn't stand up in the soft, muddy ground and just fell back down.

A corn field in the Lapaterique Mountains of Honduras, where Chico lives.

Chico watched his papa stand up another corn plant, only to see it tumble back to the wet earth. Papa snatched up the stalk and threw it as far as he could! Papa picked up a rock and threw it at the stalk! Chico quickly leaped behind a tree before his papa could see him. He felt uncomfortable, as though he were spying on Papa.

Papa dropped to his knees and sobbed, "Why? Why? Why? What have I done? Why do you torment us so?"

Chico didn't know to whom his papa was talking. He had never seen his papa cry. Papa had told him many times, "Strong men don't cry." Even when Chico had fallen and hurt his knee, his papa had told him not to cry.

Chico hurried back to the house without his papa seeing him. Rosa was hanging the damp sheets on the fence to dry when Chico ran in to the back of the house.

"Where is your papa?" questioned Mama.

"Still in the fields," mumbled Chico. He didn't want anyone to know that he had seen his papa so upset.

Mama handed a warm tortilla to Chico. He laid it flat in his palm as Mama spooned refried beans into it. She handed him a cup of sweet, warm coffee. Folding his tortilla and beans in half, Chico sat down on the floor in the corner beside the sacks of beans and corn. He slowly let the food warm his belly.

Papa's presence filled the doorway and blocked out the light and warmth of the sunshine. Seeing his papa so upset about the corn had left Chico feeling sick inside. Chico didn't want his papa to know that he had seen Papa crying in the corn field.

Chico shoved himself further back into the corner and tried to become invisible. Mama quickly put a plate of food on the table in front of Papa. Papa slumped down in the chair and began to eat.

"How are the fields?" asked Mama.

"Gone!" was all Papa croaked out.

"Is nothing at all left?" Mama asked hopefully.

"I said it is GONE!" Papa slammed his fist down on the table.

Mama didn't say another word but went to the half-full sacks of beans sitting on the floor beside Chico. She pushed down on the sacks in the corner to see how much of the beans and corn were left inside. Chico thought he saw a tear on her sad face.

Walking around outside later in the day Chico realized that the storm had damaged more than just the corn. The roof on the school had been blown half off. The little bridge into Reitoca had been washed away. The road into town had slid off the side of the hill. Now no trucks with supplies for the people could enter until someone did some work on the road and bridge.

Chico and his family lived on the edge of the town of Reitoca *(Re-a-TO-ka)* in the Lapaterique *(Lay-pa-te-REE-kay)* Mountains of Honduras. Reitoca was a long way from anywhere. Large mountains on all sides surrounded the little town. Once a week a truck bringing supplies would travel over the mountains from the paved road. Chico's papa and the other papas would sell their crops to the truck driver. Chico never had seen the paved road. People said walking the road took seven hours. Don Felix had a little store in which people could buy soap, candles, salt, machetes, rubber boots, and other items the trucks brought.

An adobe house like the one where Chico and his family live in Reitoca, Honduras.

Chico's house was a made of adobe bricks with a tin roof. The little house had two rooms. One room had a large wooden bed where Mama and Papa slept. Both rooms had hard-packed, dirt floors. The rooms had no door between them—just a large opening. Chickens pecked around in the yard and spent their nights in the tree. Pigs wandered

16

around the houses. Behind the wooden front door hung a long string of garlic. Chico's mama said that the garlic would protect them from evil spirits. The garlic had worked well up until the storm had hit. Chico's family didn't have much money, but it had what it needed. Every day Chico and his brothers and sisters and their parents ate tortillas made from the corn they grew. This was their bread. They ate rice and beans almost every day. Occasionally they had eggs or chicken. Sometimes they would sell eggs. A man in Reitoca had a cow and made white cheese from the milk. They would use money they made from selling eggs to buy cheese or other things they needed.

The men of Reitoca planted beans and corn on the sides of the mountains outside of town. They would leave for the fields before the sun rose. Every day before they went to school, Chico and the other boys would take breakfast to their papas in the fields.

Chico would meet up with his best friend, Rafael, and walk to school together. They would pass the little Catholic church with the padlock on it. About once a year a priest arrived to open it up and have a church service. Mama and lots of women always went, but Papa never did. The next town had another little church in it, but the boys never had been to it. They would pass the health center. It also was locked up. None of the boys ever could remember seeing a nurse or doctor.

A few days after the storm, classes started back at school. Chico liked school. He liked running with his friends and playing soccer at recess. He liked the stories his teacher told. He liked saying the sounds of the letters and reading with all the other children.

After school all the boys from Reitoca either would play soccer or go to the creek to swim. Chico's friend, Rafael, was a good kid. He always obeyed and did the right thing.

He never got in trouble. José, another friend, was tall and really could kick the soccer ball a long way. Calvin lived close by but really wasn't a friend. He was a little older than the rest of the boys and always tried to push everyone around. He always wanted to pick a fight. Chico was a little scared of Calvin. Pedro and Jorge lived close by, too. Lots of boys were in Reitoca. Chico always had someone as a companion.

The storm changed everything. The men had no reason to work in the corn fields. The corn was gone. So now Chico didn't take his papa breakfast in the field before school.

Not long after the storm, the chickens began to die. Mama burned a candle the night the first chicken died and prayed to the saints to keep the other chickens from dying. The next day more chickens died. The saints must not have been listening, because soon afterward, all the chickens died. He would sure miss having eggs. *A fried egg on a fresh hot tortilla is so good,* thought Chico. Mama had sold some of the eggs and used the money to buy things such as sugar, coffee, and candles that they needed. Without the money Mama made from selling the eggs, she ran out of coffee and sugar quickly.

The storm even changed school. The three classes in their little school combined into one big class. Miss Gonzales and Miss Perez would not continue teaching. The families with whom they had been living no longer could feed them, so they were going to move back to their homes in the capital city. Miss Alvarez was to teach all three classes together. At least the school hadn't closed completely.

Each day Mama gave Chico fewer beans on his tortilla. Each day Papa grew more frustrated. Chico missed the sweet coffee each morning, but at least he had a warm, corn tortilla for breakfast with a small amount of refried beans inside. Chico used to get hungry right before lunch time, but now he got hungry in the middle of the morning. That hungry feeling turned into a pain in the pit of his stomach. After school, none of the boys wanted to play soccer. They just didn't have the energy. So they sat around under the shade trees and talked.

A few days later the bean sack in the corner lay flat on the floor. The sack of beans went empty; so did Chico's belly. The next day Mama gave Chico a tortilla for breakfast, but no beans were on it. No beans, no rice, no eggs. Tortillas—nothing but tortillas; even they didn't have much taste anymore. The constant hunger made Chico feel as though he had a hole burning in the middle of his belly. He didn't seem to have energy to do anything. He got tired walking down to the creek to take a bath. He got tired sitting under the trees with his friends talking. He was just tired all the time.

One morning Chico awoke to a quiet house. The fire was out. Not having a fire going in the kitchen felt strange. Mama sat at the table with her head in her hands. The family had no more corn. That meant no more tortillas. No tortillas!

Every house in the little town of Reitoca was the same. All the other kids in town were hungry, also. The pain in Chico's belly always was there. He was hungry, but Chico didn't complain, because he knew everyone else in his family was hungry, too. Baby Lupe cried almost all the time. His little brother, Abel, slept most of the day. His little sister, Nanci, whined and fussed. Chico wanted to scream, but he didn't; he was strong. Chico wondered what would happen to them. Would they get sick because they didn't have enough food to keep them healthy? If they got sick, would they die? They needed food to stay alive. They had to have some food, but how?

One day Mama called Chico and said, "Your papa is taking our pig into the big town to sell it, so we can buy some beans and corn for tortillas. Chico, I want you to go to your Aunt Sara's. Maybe the storm did not destroy their crops, since they live on the other side of the mountains. Perhaps they can help us."

Chico's eyes grew big, "That's in Porvenir (POOR-ve-near)! That's a long way. I can't go by myself!"

Papa entered and yelled, "You can, and you will!"

Chico looked up into his Papa's dark eyes and saw the anger. Chico swallowed hard and was too scared of Papa to say another word.

Mama softly said, "Take the road. It is a longer walk, but you can stay at people's houses along the way."

"What? He is not a baby!" boomed Papa. "He has to learn to be a man. He can go over the mountains. It is quicker. A man is not afraid of staying in the mountains."

Chico had been to Aunt Sara's before but never by himself. It was a two-day walk over a lonely, winding, steep trail.

The next morning the sun was just barely peeking over the mountain when Chico tied a gourd full of water to his belt. His mama gave him a hug and a backpack with a hammock in it. "Be careful, my son." She said, "Tie your hammock high up on the trees tonight. Wild pigs might be up in the mountains. You also could . . . " She faded the sentence off and did not finish it. But Chico knew what she meant. Then she continued, "If I had a candle, I would light it. I would pray to the saints to look after for you. But we don't have money to buy a candle. Just take care, my son."

Chico began the long trip up and over the mountain. He really liked his Aunt Sara. She and Uncle Alin were different from most people. They were so kind and helpful. He would enjoy seeing them again. The walk would have been nice if Chico's belly hadn't been hurting so. Oh, how he dreamed of a tortilla filled with beans! He stopped under a big rubber tree. The shade felt so good. He slowly sipped the water in his gourd and watched the vultures circling overhead. He thought, *They will be circling for me and my family if Aunt Sara doesn't have any food for us.*

Chico wished he were running and playing soccer with friends like he did several months before. He looked off in the distance and recognized the big, flat rocks that balanced on two sandstone pedestals. They were called the Drum Rocks. People said that the old Lenca Indians had used the Drum Rocks as a special religious place. *My great-great-grandfathers used to go to the Drum Rock; now Mama just lights candles to the saints.*

The trail that Chico travels over the mountains.

Chico got up and continued on the path over the mountains. He passed tall trees that provided nice shade for his walk. He passed tall, grassy areas, where he wondered if a snake might be hiding. He crossed tiny, little streams of water that he could just step across. Then at one of the larger streams Chico refilled his gourd and sat for a while under the shade tree with his feet in the water. The water ran across the little pebbles and glistened in the sun. Tadpoles darted at the edge of the water.

He remembered a few years ago when he had traveled this same trail with his whole family. Baby Lupe hadn't been born yet nor had his little brother, Abel. Nanci had been a small baby at that time. Mama had used a big cloth to tie Nanci on her back. Things had been so different then. They had stopped at this very spot and played in the water. Mama had given them cold beans wrapped in tortillas and big hunks of salty, white cheese to eat. Thinking about food made Chico's belly ache worse. Aunt Sara's oldest son, Wesli, had gotten married. What a feast they had—baked chickens, roasted pig, and white, fluffy rice!

Oh, I must stop thinking about food! Chico said out loud to no one but himself. He picked up his backpack. He started on up the mountain. Darkness soon would fall. He needed to go as far as he could before dark. Chico scouted out two trees just the right distance apart to hang his hammock, as the sun began to set behind the mountain. He found a big rock and stood on it to tie his hammock as high as he could. Wild pigs were not something he wanted to mess with. He found a big, strong stick. He might need it to defend himself in the night.

The stars began to twinkle in the sky. Chico lay back in his hammock. He remembered Mama's warnings to be careful. He knew that wild pigs were not the only things she was worried about getting Chico. He had heard about mountain cougars but never had seen one. Chico's heart raced a little just thinking about the possibilities. He heard an owl hooting; he jumped. He heard the night hawks calling out a gentle, "Wick, wick, wheeoooo. Wick wick wheeoooo." The full moon cast scary shadows. A cool breeze whistled through the trees; Chico forced his heart to slow down to a normal beat.

As Chico began to drift off to sleep, he suddenly heard a rustling sound in the nearby bushes. His heart jumped up into his throat. *Tha dum, tha dum,* loudly beat his heart. *Tha dum, tha dum.*

Chico had to strain to hear. *What was that noise?* Wild pigs could rip the flesh off his bones in minutes. Mountain cougars would claw and chew him to death.

A typical kitchen, such as the one where Aunt Sara
serves Chico rice, beans, and tortillas.

T W O

Aunt Sara's

*

Because of his pounding heart Chico could barely hear exactly where the sound was from. He scampered up one end of the hammock until he was almost climbing up the rope. In the stream of moonlight, as he peeked around the leaves of the tree, he saw the bushes moving! What was out there? Out scampered a pair of possums. The mama possum had about six little babies clinging to her back. Chico thought to himself, *Boy, am I silly, being scared by little bitty possums!*

Chico finally drifted off to a restless sleep. He awoke several times during the night. He listened intently to the sounds of the forest around him. This was the longest night of his life. *Will the sun ever rise?* wondered Chico several times in the night.

Soon things were light enough to see the path. He untied his hammock, stuffed it in his backpack, and started down the trail. Up and down the trail he went. A little, green, grass snake slithered across the trail and into some bushes. By mid-morning he felt as if his legs were like heavy rocks. He was afraid to sit down and rest—afraid that if he sat down, he would not be able to force his legs to stand back up.

The sun reached the middle of the sky. Chico arrived at a small group of houses. He swayed slightly on his worn-out feet. He could hardly stand up because of the gnawing hunger. Lack of food and exhaustion clouded his thoughts. He couldn't remember exactly where Aunt Sara's house was.

Out front at the second house he saw a boy about his age.

"Can you tell me where Sara and Alin Dominquez live?" Chico asked.

"Yeah, they live at the far side of the little town, past the little Christian church," the boy replied. "What's your name? Where are you from? Are you okay? You look kind of funny." The boy bombarded Chico with questions.

"I haven't eaten in a long time. I don't feel so good, but I can make it that far."

"I will walk with you and carry your pack," responded the boy as he took the lightweight pack with just a hammock in it from Chico's shoulders.

"Thanks," said Chico. He felt as if a ton of rock had been taken from him.

The boy chattered as he and Chico went. "That is our school." He pointed to a small building. "And that is the health center," he said, as he pointed to an even smaller building. "We have a nurse that visits our town every week and works in the clinic," the boy said. "She gave me a shot once. I didn't even cry," he boasted.

"See that big tree?" Marvin went on. "We climb it all the time. One time my little brother fell out of it and broke his arm. The nurse had to set it; it's okay now, but my little brother wants us to feel sorry for him, so sometimes he acts like it still hurts."

Chico's head hurt. He felt so tired, he could hardly pay attention to all the boy was saying.

The boy babbled on, "Over there is where the school teacher lives. Over there is the mayor's house." The boy pointed to the different houses. "Behind the mayor's house are some orange trees. He lets us pick the oranges. They are real juicy.

"Up there is our Christian church. The pastor lives next door. You will have to go there sometime while you are visiting. It is so much fun. We sing lots of songs. The pastor tells us stories from the Bible. Have you ever been to church?" asked the boy.

"No," responded Chico. He had no energy left to tell the boy that his town had no church—only the Catholic church with the padlock on it.

"That house over there is your Aunt Sara's," the boy said, as he pointed a short distance. "You better sit down. You don't look so good. I'll run on up there and tell her you are here."

Chico sat down on a big rock and leaned his throbbing head against the nearby tree. He closed his eyes.

When he next opened them, he was lying on the ground. Someone was putting a cool cloth on his head and calling his name. Slowly he began to make sense of things. It was his Aunt Sara. "Chico, Chico," she called. She was patting him. "Here, drink some of this." She placed a glass up to his lips. *Milk!* thought Chico, *with sugar in it. Ahh, it tastes so rich and sweet.*

Chico slowly sat up and looked around. He saw the chatty boy who had shown him the way. He saw his Aunt Sara and two other kids he didn't know. They were all staring at him with wide-open eyes. Aunt Sara said, "Get up slowly." She put her arm around him. So did the talkative boy. They helped Chico walk up to the house.

Once inside the house, Aunt Sara said, "I think you need to rest, but first, drink some more sweet milk. After you rest some, you can tell me why you are here. Here, lie down on my bed."

Chico was so weary; the sweet milk tasted so good as it stopped the burning pain in his belly, he could do nothing but obey. After a short nap Chico awoke. Aunt Sara sat nearby in a rocking chair.

"Do you feel better now?" she asked.

"Yes, thank you," whispered Chico as he sat up in the bed.

"I am so happy to see you," Aunt Sara said, "but tell me why you traveled so far and all alone."

"I was sent by my mama and papa," began Chico. "We have no food. I had not eaten anything for several days before I got here. We had a big storm. The wind blew over all the corn. We had small sacks of beans and corn, but they all are gone. Mama and Papa sent me to get help. Can you help us?"

"Yes, of course," she answered as she reached out and ruffled Chico's dark hair. Aunt Sara's kind response was like a big, heavy weight lifted from Chico. He breathed a sign of relief.

"Why are you so kind?" the question popped out of Chico's mouth.

Aunt Sara's caring eyes looked at him. "Because God loves me," she replied. Seeing Chico's puzzled expression at her words, she continued, "Sit here in the kitchen. I will fix you some rice and beans while I tell you about Jesus."

Chico followed her into the kitchen. "Have I heard about Jesus?" Chico asked. "Isn't he one of the saints? My mama lights candles and prays to the saints."

"No," she responded, "Jesus is God's own Son." Aunt Sara began speaking slowly as if gathering her thoughts as she spoke. "You see, God loves us so much that He sent His Son, Jesus, to show us how much He cares about us."

Chico accepted the plate of beans, rice, and tortillas from Aunt Sara. The smell of the beans and rice made Chico's mouth water.

He watched the way the little red beans covered the white rice. The bean juice ran through, flavoring the rice. The slightly sweet smell of the corn tortilla was so familiar, it made him think of his mama. He wondered if she had any tortillas to eat. If Papa had sold the pig, maybe he had bought some corn for the family. Chico took a bite of the mixture of beans and rice and felt warmth run through his body.

"Jesus is God's Son," continued Sara. "Jesus came to earth as a baby, born to the Virgin Mary."

"I know about Christmas," Chico said, as he nodded his head up and down. "And my mama sometimes lights a candle and prays to the Virgin Mary."

"Yes, Chico, I used to do the same thing until I knew Jesus," Sara said quietly. "Jesus entered the world as a baby, but He grew up and did some astonishing things."

"Like what?" asked Chico.

"He healed people and taught about God and how God wants people to live," responded Sara.

"Jesus knew how to use herbs to cure people?"

"Oh, no! He had power to just touch people; they got well!"

"I would have liked to have seen that," said Chico thoughtfully as he chewed on his tortilla.

"Me, too," replied Sara.

Balancing a large bucket of water on her head, Brendita, Chico's cousin, entered the kitchen; she had been to the river to bring water for them to use in the kitchen. Aunt Sara helped her sit the bucket on the floor.

Brendita said, "I see you feel better. You had us scared; I prayed that God would help you. I'm glad you're okay."

"Thanks," responded Chico.

"Brendita," said Aunt Sara, "Please run over and tell Marvin that Chico is doing better. He showed Chico where our house was and was worried about him."

"Sure, I'll go right away," she said as she left.

Chico's tummy felt so full! He was feeling so comfortable, yet his mind was thinking about what Sara was saying.

"Thank you, Aunt Sara, for the food," he told Aunt Sara. "So what was so important about this Saint Jesus?" he asked her.

"Remember, He was God's Son. God sent Him to save us from our sins."

"Sins?" asked Chico.

"The bad things that people do," replied Aunt Sara.

"I don't do bad things," responded Chico.

"Everyone has some bad things they do. Jesus was the only person that never sinned. He never did anything bad."

"So what else did Jesus do?" Chico asked.

"Well, He taught people about God and how to live. But some people didn't like what Jesus was teaching. So they plotted to have Him killed. They took him to a judge. He ordered them to hang Him on a cross until He died."

"So He did become a Saint," insisted Chico.

"No, remember I told you He was God's Son. After He died, God raised Him from the dead."

"Oh, wow, so He didn't stay dead! So where is He today?" asked Chico.

Bursting in to the room, the chatty boy sang out, "No, He didn't die. He lives in my heart. Hi, again. I'm glad to see you are all better."

30

Sara smiled and ruffled the boy's hair. "Chico, you have already met Marvin. He is our friend. He lives on the other side of our town."

Chico was wondering how a man could live inside another person. *Did he say that Jesus lived in his heart or throat?* thought Chico. Marvin was talking again, so he couldn't ask Aunt Sara.

"Marvin, why don't you boys go outside and visit? Just don't go far, since Chico still needs to rest."

"Hey, let's go climb the tree," shouted Marvin as he took off running toward the big tree that he had pointed out earlier to Chico.

Chico walked behind thinking about what Aunt Sara had said. *A dead man getting up and walking about. Sounds kind of scary. Must be something like a ghost*, thought Chico. He felt much better after eating but still didn't feel like running. He could climb the tree, but he didn't want to do much.

From the boys' perch high in the tree Marvin began to tell Chico about everyone in the little town. He told him how many kids each had, who was married to whom, and who was family to whom. Chico also found out that Marvin had some family living in Reitoca. Chico's friend, José, was Marvin's cousin.

Finally, Marvin slowed down talking. Chico was able to ask, "What did you mean that Jesus lived in your uh, uh, throat?"

Laughing, Marvin replied, "Not throat; in my heart! In my heart! Really, it is that part of me that thinks and feels. One day I prayed to God and asked Him to forgive my sins. I asked Jesus to enter my heart."

"Oh," said Chico, trying not to look too ignorant. He heard his Aunt Sara calling him. "Hey, I gotta go," said Chico as he climbed down.

"Okay," said Marvin. "I'll see you at church tonight."

"How do you know I'll be there?" asked Chico.

"Your Aunt Sara and Uncle Alin are always there," stated Marvin as he climbed down.

"Okay, see you," said Chico.

Sure enough, Aunt Sara said they were going to go to the church. Chico washed up. He put on a set of clean shorts that Aunt Sara gave him that used to belong to his cousin, Wesli, but Wesli had outgrown them years ago. *What would Papa say about all this Jesus stuff? Would he approve of Chico going to church? What about Mama; what would she think? Was she praying to the saints, right now?*

At church Chico clapped along with all the singing. Sitting on the wooden bench with Aunt Sara on one side of him and cousin Brendita on the other, he felt very comfortable. He did not know the words to the songs, but the singing was enjoyable. A man at the front asked the people if they needed prayer for anything.

Aunt Sara stood up and said, "My nephew arrived today. He was sent here by my sister, Margarita. They live in Reitoca over the mountain. They had a big storm a few weeks back. It destroyed their corn and bean crops. They are hungry. Please pray for them and the little town of Reitoca."

Then all the people closed their eyes bowed their heads. The man up front prayed to God and asked for help for the little town of Reitoca.

Tears sprang to his eyes. Chico swallowed. He began to think, *What is happening in Reitoca? Are Mama and Papa okay? What about the baby, Lupe? Abel? Nanci? Rosa? I feel better; I've had something to eat, but what about them. Are they still hungry?*

THREE

Help Arrives

*

Uncle Alin tied up Chico's hammock to the wooden beams in the house and said, "Chico, tomorrow the pastor and some men will be by here. We'll talk about how we can help your family and all the people in Reitoca."

"I really wanted to try to go home tomorrow," said Chico.

"You need a day of rest. I will meet with the pastor and the men. We'll make a plan on how we can help you."

Chico didn't know what else to say, but his face showed he was worried about his family.

"Don't worry," Uncle Alin continued. "We will pray for God to take care of your family."

"Here," offered Aunt Sara. "Drink some more milk before you go to sleep."

Chico accepted the warm, sweet milk sprinkled with cinnamon. He sipped the milk and felt its warmth drop from his mouth to his throat to his tummy. He took a deep breath and breathed in the soothing scent of the cinnamon.

The warm milk soon made him sleepy. Chico's aching, tired muscles relaxed. He dropped off to sleep swinging slightly in his hammock.

The next morning Aunt Sara fed Chico a fine breakfast of fried eggs and tortillas. Marvin stopped by right after breakfast.

"Hey, let's go to the creek and swim," invited Marvin.

Marvin looked up to Aunt Sara. She nodded her head *yes.* "You both need a bath."

"Great! Let's go," continued Marvin. "A tree hangs over the creek, right over the spot that is the deepest. We can jump out of the tree. Some of the women will be up creek washing clothes. My mother is there washing our clothes. So is my grandmother. You can meet them. Some of the other boys from our little town will be there, also."

Marvin continued to talk as the boys walked the path to the creek. They climbed up into the tree and jumped out into the cool creek water.

Chico met Marvin's mother and many of the other women. Marvin's mother gave the boys a bar of soap to scrub themselves. The boys scrubbed down and put plenty of soap in their hair—so much soap that their hair stood up in little poky spikes. They snickered at each other's funny looking, bubbly white hair. Then they made beards out of the soap bubbles. Laughing at each other, they began a splash war. Chico laughed, played, and forgot his worries for a while.

The boys walked back to the house. Marvin continued chatting about everything in the world. He talked about his church, his school, and anything that popped into his mind. Approaching the house, Chico saw the pastor and two men shaking Uncle Alin's hand as they left.

"Hey, boys, how was the creek?" greeted Uncle Alin.

"Wet!" giggled Marvin.

"What did you decide?" questioned Chico with worry creeping into his voice.

"The pastor is going to send someone to Reitoca to help you," responded Uncle Alin.

"My brothers and sisters can't last long. Is it someone from here? How soon will he arrive? Who will you send? How will he get there? Will they bring food? When? Who?" blurted out Chico anxiously.

"Calm down," comforted Uncle Alin, laying his hand on Chico's shoulder. "I don't know when he will get there, but you can believe that help will arrive."

Taking a deep breath Chico slowly asked, "How will we know it is the help you sent?"

"You will know because it will be a man in a green Jeep." *Green Jeep*? thought Chico.

Aunt Sara stepped into the room and said, "Boys, good news. I just talked with Marvin's mother. He can go with you halfway back to Reitoca. He can spend the night with you and walk back the next day. I'll send some food. You can picnic along the way."

"Great," smiled Chico, "and if the wild pigs bother us, Marvin can talk them away!" Everyone broke into laughter.

Early the next morning Chico and Marvin started walking the path. Chico noticed how much better he felt than when he had walked down the path just two days ago. He was not as worried and scared as he had been, plus he had a tummy full of good food. He had a backpack full of beans. His hammock was tied up on top.

Marvin had a backpack with his hammock. Inside Marvin's backpack he had some boiled eggs and some tortillas with beans rolled up inside. Of course, Marvin began the trip talking. He told Chico the names of all the trees and whether they produced fruit to eat and what time of the year they gave their fruit. Chico was glad for the company.

35

Marvin was great entertainment.

After a while Marvin stepped on Chico's shadow. He yelled, "I'm stepping on you!" Chico quickly jumped and moved his shadow into the shade of a tree.

Running toward Marvin's shadow Chico hollered back, "I'll step on you!"

For several minutes they chased each others' shadows up and over the hill. Worn out and sweating after their

A Honduran hillside, such as the one in which Chico and Marvin spend the night.

game, they sat in the shade of a big tree. Chico offered Marvin water out of his gourd. Marvin took a big drink.

"How do you know that Jesus went into your heart when you prayed?" Chico asked.

Marvin grinned and replied, "I could feel it. I felt clean; I felt like a new person. Plus it's a promise God made in the Bible—that if you ask Him, He will enter your heart and help you every day."

"Help you do what?"

"To do what is right, to be a nicer kid, to not to be afraid. Plus He will take you to his home in heaven when you die. Heaven is a wonderful place. Everyone will have a big house with lots of food."

Chico thought that would be very nice. Lots of food and no more pain in his belly.

"Let's get going again," said Chico, as he thought about what Marvin had been saying.

Late in the afternoon they passed the place where Chico had spent the night. He smiled as he remembered the possums, but he didn't tell Marvin how scared he had been. Chico knew real men weren't supposed to be scared, but he sure seemed to be worried and scared a lot of the time.

As the darkness began to creep up over the mountains, the boys searched for a nice place to make camp. Marvin had matches and built a fire, while Chico tied the hammocks up as high as he could.

After the nice supper of tortillas and beans, Chico asked, "Are you worried about the wild pigs and mountain cougars?"

"No! God will take care of us," responded Marvin confidently. "But I certainly am going to tie my hammock up as high as I can," he laughed.

Marvin continued, "Before we go to sleep, I will pray for us."

Marvin knelt down by the fire and began to pray. Chico didn't want to look dumb, so he knelt down with him. Marvin talked to God just like he talked to Chico! He asked for God to protect them from all the wild things in the forest. He asked God to help them rest and for Chico to understand about God. Marvin really could talk! He talked to God until Chico's knees hurt from the little pebbles on the ground digging into them.

As they climbed into the hammocks, Chico didn't feel worried about the wild pigs or mountain cougars. The boys talked a while until Marvin's constant steam of talk slowed down. Chico wondered, *Maybe God does care and is helping me not to be so worried or scared.* He slowly nodded off.

Chico awoke to birds singing and the sun shining. Marvin already was awake and toasting tortillas on a rock beside the fire. He motioned for Chico to get a hot tortilla. He reached into his backpack and pulled out boiled eggs. As Chico peeled his egg, he thought, *This is the way to live.* No feeling afraid, nice food, and no Papa to yell at him. He wanted to remember this moment for the rest of his life.

Now the boys had to go separate ways. Chico had to continue on. Marvin had to return home to Porvenir. They put out the fire by throwing dirt on it.

Marvin said, "I will pray for you as you walk the rest of the way home."

"Thanks for being with me. It's been great fun."

"See ya," said Marvin. He waved as he began heading back the way the boys had traveled.

"See ya," replied Chico as he picked up his backpack. He really would miss Marvin and his babbling.

The trail seemed to go by rather fast. Early in the afternoon Chico saw the roofs of the houses in Reitoca. He passed by the fields where corn should have been ready to pick. The dried, brown stalks lay on the ground.

Chico wondered what he would find at home. Would Papa have sold the pig? Would Mama and the children have had any food? Would Papa be angry at Chico for not returning yesterday? What would Papa say about Chico having gone to a church?

Chico passed his friend Rafael's house. Rafael and his brother just sat out front doing nothing. They waved at Chico.

As he neared his house, he noticed a small stream of smoke emerging from the kitchen. That meant Mama had been cooking. A smile crept across Chico's face. Papa must have sold the pig and bought food.

Mama greeted Chico with a hug. So did Rosa and all the other kids. Chico gave Mama the bag of beans. She accepted it with a big smile.

"Where is Papa?" asked Chico.

"He is out back of the house in the hammock. He sold the pig and bought us some beans, rice, corn, and salt. Rosa, call your Papa so he can hear about Chico's trip."

When everyone was together, Chico began to tell them about his trip. He left out the part about being so scared the first night and being startled by the possums. He did tell about fainting and about the chatty boy—his new friend, Marvin. Everyone agreed that Marvin sounded like fun. Chico told them about what Aunt Sara had said about Jesus. He told them about the church service and the people praying for them. He told them that the pastor and men would be sending help.

Papa listened quietly, but his jaw tightened up when Chico talked about God and the church.

When Chico finished talking, Papa said, "How do we know they really are going to send someone?"

"Oh, they will; they said they would send a man in a green Jeep. And I believed them. They are good and nice people. They are Christians."

"Well, Chico, that is fine and good for them. But we don't need a church; we need food." Papa frowned, "Don't get your hopes up. They may never arrive," he said as he walked out of the house.

Two days passed. Chico spent most of every day sitting under the big tree in the middle of the little town. He and and his friends did nothing except sit about and talk.

Chico bragged to all his friends about his trip. He told them all about Marvin and the church. He told them about the man in the green Jeep visiting, but they didn't believe him either. He told them about the game of stepping on each others' shadow. They laughed. Rafael said someday they might play that game with their shadows, but right now they didn't have the energy.

On the third day Chico and all his friends were lying on the ground by the big tree when they heard the sound of a truck. It was a different sound from the big trucks that usually travel through their town. All of a sudden a green Jeep with a rack on top of it drove through town. The kids had not seen a car of any kind in a long time. They jumped up and began to chase after it.

It stopped near the big tree in the center of town. When anything important happened, everyone gathered under this big tree to talk about it. A white man got out of the green Jeep. So did the pastor of Aunt Sara and Uncle Alin's little church. The man in the green Jeep had on a straw, wide-brimmed hat. He had kind, brown eyes and had a beard! The only man with a beard in Reitoca was an old man that lived alone on the edge of town. The man in the green Jeep had on sturdy work boots and had a knife in a leather case on his belt. All the men in the little town appeared at the tree to see what was happening. The boys climbed on the rack on the top of the green Jeep. Chico made faces at himself in the mirrors on the sides of the green Jeep. The other boys laughed. Soon everyone was making funny faces. Every boy tried to outdo the other in making the funniest face.

The man in the green Jeep talked with the men of Reitoca. They discussed the need for food and the storm that destroyed all the crops. They talked about all the needs of the little town. After the meeting the man in the green Jeep shook everyone's hands. He promised to return. He then shook all the boys' hands. He even shook Chico's hand!

Two days later Chico heard the sounds of a truck. Running outside Chico saw the green Jeep again! It was full of sacks of rice, beans, corn, and jugs of oil. Everyone made a big, long line. The man in the green Jeep gave each family a small bag of beans, rice, corn, and a bottle of oil.

The green Jeep as it heads out to help the people of Reitoca.

Chico proudly helped his papa carry the food into the house. When Mama saw what they brought, she cried tears of joy at seeing the wonderful gift. That night Chico ate until his tummy couldn't hold any more. Chico's mother smiled at him. Her smile made Chico feel warm inside.

The next day the man from the green Jeep pulled out of the Jeep shovels, hoes, and wheelbarrows. He promised to pay the people in food for work they would do. All the papas began working to repair the road. The road really needed work. Sometimes the trucks couldn't get through because of the mud.

That night everyone met under the big tree. The men of the little town met with the man in the green Jeep. They talked about how they could get seeds for the next year's crop. The man in the green Jeep told the men that he would help them.

As they finished the meeting, some of the men asked the man in the green Jeep why he would help them. Chico stopped playing just to hear what the man said: "Because God loves me and loves you. God sent his Son, Jesus, down to earth to show His love for you. God has sent me to help you and teach you about Jesus."

Every week the man in the green Jeep returned and brought more food and talked with the men. They planned ways to get ready to plant the beans. They talked about the work on the road they were doing. They also talked about Jesus, God's Son. Standing around the edge of the circle of the men Chico and the other boys heard the man in the green Jeep explain how Jesus had entered the world to show people what God was like. Jesus was there to forgive them for the bad things they had done. He asked the men if any of them wanted to know Jesus. If so, they could pray with him. Several people including Rafael's papa moved forward and knelt down to pray. Chico looked at his papa, but Papa gritted his teeth and stood where he was.

The people in the little town of Reitoca began to meet together in Don Felix's house. They sang songs, read the Bible, and prayed together. Chico wondered if this was God showing his love to the little town of Reitoca through the man in the green Jeep.

Soon the time to plant beans arrived. The man in the green Jeep bought bean seeds and gave some to each family. He told each family that when the harvest arrived, they would have to pay back the seeds. Chico's papa said that everyone would pay back the seeds.

Chico and his papa worked every day in the fields. They chopped down all the weeds and then burned the field. They planted bean seeds. The beans plants needed sunshine and rain to make them grow. They had plenty of sunshine, but since the big storm, not much rain had fallen.

Chico couldn't wait for the beans to grow in the field. He remembered how delicious the new, fresh-picked beans tasted.

One day Chico was sweaty and thirsty as he entered the house. Sitting on the kitchen table was a little stand made from a tree branch. It held the glasses made out of gourds. Chico grabbed the brightly painted clay rooster water pitcher, but it was empty. The buckets that Chico's mama and sister brought back from the creek every morning also were empty. *No water again. This happened yesterday, also.*

Chico lifted the empty bucket and yelled to Rosa to help him bring back more water. Rosa slowly dragged her feet and whined, "I went this morning. I don't want to walk all the way to the creek again! It's too hot!" Their mama overheard the conversation and said, "Hush, now! Both of you take a bucket and bring back water. We must have water for supper."

So Chico grabbed two buckets and walked out with Rosa following him. Rosa picked up the *jacal* (HA-cal), a gourd-like bowl, to scoop up the water. As they walked to the creek, Rosa said softly with changed attitude, "Thank you for carrying my bucket to the creek for me." Chico replied, "No problem. I'm just sorry that you will have to carry it back so far when it will be full and heavy." Rosa responded, "Well, I do it every day and sometimes two times a day."

The walk to the creek was hot and dusty. When they got to the creek, it had just a tiny trickle of water. They walked up the creek a ways. The little bit of water felt cool on their dusty hot feet. They splashed the cool water on their legs. At the side of the hill the water dripped out of the ground. Rosa placed the *jacal* under the trickle and splashed the water up on her face. Chico sat down in the water. He stretched out in the shallow stream and let it flow over his sweaty face. Rosa sat on the bank watching him.

"What's wrong, Rosa?" he asked.

"The creek is so low. Every day it has less water. What will we do if it dries up completely?"

Chico just sat there looking at her and didn't know how to reply. Each time the *jacal* was full of water, Rosa poured it into the bucket until both buckets were full. They carried the water back to the house. Rosa carefully balanced her bucket on her head the way all Honduran women carry heavy loads. Chico carried his on his shoulder the way Honduran men carry heavy items. No one taught them how to carry things this way; that was just the way things were done.

Later that evening, Chico, Rosa and their whole family walked down the path to the Felix family's house that people used for a church in the little town of Reitoca. Chico asked his papa the same question that Rosa had asked him earlier.

"What will we we do if the creek dries up completely?" Chico's papa just shrugged his shoulders and shook his head.

At Don Felix's house Mama and the children went inside. Papa stood around outside the window with several other men and pretended not to listen. The people inside sang a song about rivers of living water. Don Felix told a story about a woman who went to a well and met Jesus

44

there. Jesus told her that He had water and that if she drank it, she never would be thirsty again. Boy, that sounded good to Chico! He and Rosa would not have to take the long walk to the creek again!

The next morning Chico's papa sat down at the kitchen table. He had his head down and sadly said, "If we don't get rain soon, the beans will dry up and die." Chico thought, *If the beans died, then we will have nothing to eat again.* Chico remembered when they had gone days without eating. Papa's words made Chico feel sick all over. He thought, *The beans have to have water! Will our family go hungry again? What can we do?*

The men of Reitoca meet with the man in the green Jeep, at right.

45

Reitoca men and a boy with pipes to be pounded into the side of the mountain to draw out water.

F O U R

The Well

*

A few days later the man in the green Jeep drove up over the hill. Chico and his friends were playing soccer. Seeing the green Jeep, the excited boys chased after it. Chico caught up to the Jeep just as it slowed down on the curve of the road. He jumped up on the bumper and held on to the ladder that went up to the rack on top of the Jeep. The other boys chased along behind. They shrieked and laughed at Chico.

The Jeep stopped beside the big tree in the center of town. The man got out, smiled at the boys, and shook hands with each one of them. Chico and his friends climbed up on top of the green Jeep and listened to the men talk.

After the men talked for a while, the man in the green Jeep asked the men to walk with him down to the creek. They all strolled down the creek to the place where the water barely rippled over the rocks. The men stopped and talked.

Chico and all his friends stood at the edge of the creek. Rafael picked up a big rock and threw it hard into the creek.

It splashed him and the other boys. The boys hollered and laughed. The papas scolded the boys and told them to be quiet. The men talked and walked back and forth across the hillside. They stopped frequently while they talked and pointed at the ground. They acted as though they were looking for something.

Walking back to town from the creek, Rafael saw his older sister, Virginia. She was walking slowly. The boys caught up with her.

She asked, "Is Chema with you boys?"

"What?" asked Rafael. Chico thought Chema was much older than Rafael. *Why would he be with us?* Chema wasn't his real name. His real name was José Maria, but that was just too difficult to say all at once, so everyone called him Chema.

"Is he behind you?" she asked sweetly.

"I don't know!" said Rafael as he punched Chico in the ribs and gave him a funny, questioning look.

Chico began to make his eyebrows go up and down and he giggled trying to tell Rafael without words, "She likes him!"

"Oh," said Rafael, "I get it." He said, looking around, "He is back behind us."

Virginia slowed down and acted as though she had a rock in her shoe. Chico and Rafael giggled and ran on up the path.

The following week Chico helped his papa and the other men as they built a box out of cement on the side of the hill. Chico and Rafael had to haul buckets of sand up from the creek. The men used the sand to mix with the cement from the bags that the man in the green Jeep had brought.

The next week the man in the green Jeep returned. On top of the Jeep he had several pipes. He took out the biggest hammer Chico and his friends had ever seen. The

48

boys helped carry the pipes to the side of the mountain to the very spot that the men had stopped walking the other day. Chico's papa grabbed the big hammer and swung it over his shoulder.

The men took one of the pipes and began to pound it into the side of the mountain at the spot the man in the green Jeep had pointed out. They were driving it in sideways.

Chico and the other boys watched with puzzled faces. They wondered what in the world the men were doing. The men took turns hitting the pipe with a big hammer. "Bam! Bam!" was the sound the hammer made with each hit of the pipe. The pipe only moved a few inches with each hit. It was difficult work. Once one of the pipes was almost totally in the mountain, the men screwed on another pipe and continued to drive it into the mountain.

Late in the afternoon the hot, sweaty men were so tired, they couldn't lift the heavy hammer any more. Their arms ached. They sat down under a shade tree and took drinks of water from the bucket. Chico picked up the huge hammer, but it was so big and heavy, he could barely lift it. "Hey, Rafael, help me," Chico called to his friend.

Together they tried to hit the pipe like the men had been doing. Both of the boys' strength was necessary to hit the end of the pipe. They hit it as hard as they could. They hit the pipe again. The hammer was so heavy that they couldn't even pick it up a third time. They sat down on the ground beside the pipe. Everyone was exhausted.

Chico's papa got up, spat into his hands, and rubbed them together. He took the hammer from the boys. With all his strength he swung the hammer, hitting it with a fierce blow. Everyone was holding their breath and watching. The pipe moved several inches more into the side of the mountain. A tiny trickle of water appeared.

Chico yelled, "Look, the pipe is dripping water!" The men jumped up. The men and boys began to cheer! The men who had been so tired now had energy again. They began to take turns hitting the pipe. With each pound of the hammer more and more water came out. Each one took a turn until the pipe was driven further into the hillside and a steady stream of water was pouring out.

The men jumped up and down and slapped each other on the back. They hollered. They laughed. They splashed water onto their hot but smiling faces. The concrete box tank began to fill with water. So much water was pouring out that everyone in the village could get water.

The man from the green Jeep took off his hat and bowed his head. The men took off their hats and bowed their heads. The man in the green Jeep prayed. He thanked God for giving them water that would grow plants providing food for their families.

A bean field in Reitoca.

The man from the green Jeep told the people, "Even during the dry season this spring of water still will flow. It will never run dry. It's like the spiritual water that Jesus gives our souls. It's eternal."

Chico didn't understand what the man in the green Jeep meant, but he was thrilled to have water that would never go dry. He would help his papa carry buckets to water the beans so they wouldn't die.

The man in the green Jeep continued to visit their little town of Reitoca frequently. More people began meeting for church in Don Felix's house. One night the man in the green Jeep visited and preached.

At the end of the service he asked if anyone wanted to accept Jesus as Savior. Chico's mama went to the front of the church and knelt down and prayed. Chico looked out the church window to where his papa stood. He was staring at Mama as if he had never ever seen her before.

After the service the people met together and decided to build a real church building. Don Felix's house wasn't big enough for everyone who was attending. The man in the green Jeep helped them make plans on how to build the building.

For the next several weeks each day after school the boys would go to the creek and shovel the sand. They made big piles on the side of the creek bank. The men cut straw with their long machetes and piled it on the edge of town. They were getting all the supplies ready to make adobe blocks.

One day as the boys shoveled sand, they heard the sound of trucks on the road. It was the man in the green Jeep plus another truck. Chico had never seen a truck this big.

The big truck (actually, big dump truck) backed up to the creek. When the truck stopped, out jumped the biggest man Chico had ever seen. The man in the green Jeep called him *Hermano* (Er-MA-no) Larry. Brother Larry shook each boy's hand and said, "You fellows have done a good job shoveling up the sand."

Proudly Rafael said, "I did the most!" Chico began to laugh out loud.

The other boys started laughing and yelling, "That's not true."

"Yes, I did!" Someone splashed Rafael with a shovel full of water.

The man in the green Jeep and *Hermano* Larry walked over to the creek and began splashing everyone. Refreshed, wet, and laughing they sat on the creek bank in the shade of the dump truck.

"All right, now," said *Hermano* Larry as he stood up, "we need the sand in the truck bed. Grab your shovels. We'll throw it up in there." *Hermano* Larry grabbed Rafael's shovel and began shoveling sand with the boys.

The man in the green Jeep walked up the hill and back into the little town of Reitoca. He left the boys to work with *Hermano* Larry. Throwing a shovel full of dirt up into the truck bed was difficult work. *Hermano* Larry shoveled as much as all the boys did together. When the truck was almost full *Hermano* Larry told the boys to keep working and that he would be back soon.

As *Hermano* Larry walked over the top of the hill, Chico headed for the door of the truck.

"I am going to drive this truck!" declared Chico.

The other boys chorused, "No! Don't get in it."

"No, Chico, you will get into trouble!" protested Rafael with big eyes. "Something might happen."

Chico stepped up on the step beside the door. "No, no, you better not," hollered the boys. Then, all of the sudden, Calvin, the biggest and oldest boy, jumped up on the step of the truck and knocked Chico off. He threw open the door and climbed in. "I'll show you how to drive this truck. You are just a little, scared kid." All work stopped. Everyone froze. Chico's eyes grew big. Chico was just kidding everyone. He really hadn't intended to get in the truck. Calvin was always showing off. He was meaner, stronger, and tougher than the other boys. He always was getting into trouble at school. Now Chico really was scared. What would Calvin do?

The hollering by all the boys continued. Most were telling Calvin to get out of the truck. A few told him to try and drive it. Out of the corner of his eye Chico saw José take off running toward the town. Calvin, wearing a foolish-looking smile, was sitting behind the steering wheel. He was moving the wheel back and forth making truck sounds.

Calvin reached out with his hand and pulled on the stick that stuck up from the floor. All of a sudden the truck jumped. The boys scampered away from the vehicle. Slowly it began rolling backward toward the edge of the creek. All the boys were screaming. Calvin sat with his eyes forward and screamed. The truck was moving! It rolled back into the creek and then stopped when the water was halfway up the back wheel. All the boys got real quiet. Calvin jumped out and slammed the door shut. He snarled at all the boys, "Don't anyone tell them I did it. Say the truck rolled back by itself."

He quickly scanned all the boys' faces. "If you tell I did it, I will beat you up!" All the boys who had been scared for Calvin were now scared of Calvin.

"You know I can," he threatened.

The papas ran from the town to see what all the commotion was about. The man from the green Jeep and *Hermano* Larry couldn't run as fast as the papas could. They just stood there looking at the truck, half in the water.

"Is anyone hurt?" asked the man in the green Jeep.

Shaking their heads, the boys quietly all chorused, "No."

"Well, let's get the truck out," said *Hermano* Larry as he climbed into the dump truck.

"What happened?" asked Rafael's papa. Rafael looked scared and lied, "I don't know. It just rolled back." Then Pedro and some of the other boys began, "Yeah, it just started rolling back."

Chico stared at the wheels of the truck and didn't look at his papa.

"That's odd; I know I left the brake on," said *Hermano* Larry as the engine started up. The truck began to move forward, but it just wouldn't go. *Hermano* Larry moved the sticks emerging from the floor. The engine roared. It just would not move. The back tires just spun round and round, but they didn't go anywhere.

Finally *Hermano* Larry got out and looked at the tires. "We will have to dig some of the sand out from around the tires. Then the tires will have something solid to grab on to," he announced. Several men started digging out the sand. After a long while, they finally hit the solid bottom.

"Now it'll probably pull out," said *Hermano* Larry.

He climbed back up into the truck. The truck roared and grunted and groaned and slowly pulled out of the water. When the truck made it up to the top of the creek bank, *Hermano* Larry yelled out the window, "Everyone hop on!"

All the men and boys scampered aboard. Chico climbed on top of the sand. What a view! They were up so high, they could see the creek as it wound its way down the mountain. The wind whipped across Chico's face. As they pull into Reitoca, Chico could see all the houses. This normally would have been a real thrill—his first ride in a big truck—but Chico felt funny knowing that they had not told the truth about what had happened. Chico continued to look out at the world around him in order to avoid looking at his papa. He was worried about what Papa was going to say to him when he got home.

That afternoon after *Hermano* Larry dumped the sand beside the church for the men to make the adobe blocks, Papa and Chico walked home in silence. Chico could see that Papa wasn't happy. So Chico kept real quiet. Once they were home, Papa began to yell at Chico. "What were you boys thinking? Someone could have been killed. Haven't I told you before? Don't mess with stuff that is not yours. Don't for one minute think I believed that story that the truck rolled back all by itself. You boys did something."

Chico felt guilty for pretending that he was going to drive the truck. He hung his head down. Papa went on and on, but Chico felt so bad, he didn't even hear all Papa said. All the fun of the riding in the truck had been spoiled by the terrible guilty feelings.

Finally Papa slowed down talking. Chico looked up. Suddenly Papa grabbed Chico and was going to hit him! Mama quietly walked over and said, "Let the boy go. He didn't mean any harm." Papa let go and growled, "Go sit outside. I don't even want to look at you right now."

Chico sat under the tree at the back of the house. He could hear Mama and Papa inside talking. Mama's voice was kind and sweet, but Papa's was angry. Chico knew he had done wrong.

Just then, Calvin walked by and snarled at him. "Remember!" was all he said. Chico knew what he meant.

That evening, walking to the meeting at the Felix's house, Chico wondered if this terrible feeling would ever go away. At Don Felix's Chico sat beside Rafael.

Chico whispered to him, "My papa was really angry over the truck."

"Mine, too," whispered back Rafael.

"I feel terrible," said Chico.

"Me, too," replied Rafael.

"My papa said it was a sin. He knows I lied," stated Rafael.

Chico looked up at the window. He saw Calvin watching him. Chico quickly lowered his eyes. He really was scared of Calvin.

The crowd sang several songs. Chico clapped and sang along, but his heart just wasn't in it. The man from the green Jeep talked about God forgiving people of the wrongs they do. Chico felt worse about what had happened. The man from the green Jeep asked if the people there wanted Jesus to forgive their sins and ask Jesus to enter their lives.

Chico felt very uncomfortable. Then Rafael stood up and walked forward. Was he going to tell? Rafael knelt down. The man from the green Jeep knelt beside Rafael. Chico felt warm and cold all at the same time. He glanced at the window and saw his papa. His jaw was tight like it always was when people talked about God. Standing beside his papa was Calvin staring at him.

That night after the service Chico ran all the way home. He didn't want to see or talk to anyone. He lay on his mat on the floor and couldn't sleep. Everyone in the house was asleep. All he could think about was what had happened today.

What would have happened if I had never jumped up there and pretended that I was going to get in the truck? Maybe Calvin would not have gotten in the truck. What if one of the little boys told someone what had happened? What if Papa found out that I had been bragging that I was going to drive the truck? What would Papa do then? How can I avoid Calvin? Calvin sure can hit hard, but Papa can do worse. Oh, what am I going to do?

Chico turned over on his side. *What happened to Rafael, going forward and praying like that at the meeting? Did that mean he is a Christian now?*

Chico turned over to his other side. *What is wrong with me? Why can't I just be a good kid? Rafael is a good kid. He doesn't need God to help him be good. Yeah, he lied today, but that was just to protect his skin from Calvin.*

Chico turned on to his back. *Ahh,* he screamed inside, *Why can't I just stop worrying and go to sleep? Will the man in the green Jeep return here after what happened to the dump truck?*

The men of Reitoca making adobe bricks.

For the next few weeks the men in the town worked and made adobe bricks. The boys had to haul water from the creek to help. They made a big puddle. They turned up the dirt with shovels until they had a nice, thick mud. They added straw and sand. With bare feet and rolled-up pants the boys and men jumped into the puddle. They mixed it all up by walking around and squishing it all together with their feet. The boys and men laughed. They packed the mud mixture into a square, wooden mold. They dumped the blocks out of the mold and left them to dry in the sun. The hot sun baked the adobe bricks for several weeks.

While the bricks dried, the men cleared off a spot in town for the church building. They worked to make it as level as possible. The women arrived with their brooms they had made out of tree branches and swept the dirt clean. Every day the women sprinkled water on the dirt floor and then swept it clean. This packed the dirt harder and made a packed floor.

The man in the green Jeep had not visited Reitoca in a long time. *Is he mad at us boys for what we did to the dump truck? Will he return?* wondered Chico.

For weeks everyone worked together. The women swept the dirt while the men worked on the building. The men stacked the adobe bricks and built the walls. Soon they had four walls but no roof! The men made a door out of wood. They then had four walls and a door but no roof! They built some window shutters that could open during the meetings but close off the window holes when no one was using the building. So now they had four walls, a door, and windows but no roof. They built benches. The people begin meeting in the roof-less building. They sat on their new benches, with the four walls, doors, and windows but no roof. They had done everything they could do, but they could not put the roof on, because they had no tin or nails.

Chico continued to go to the little church. He had nothing else to do. Besides he did enjoy hearing the stories about Jesus and the other people of the Bible. Best of all Chico like to sing and clap his hands with all the other people. Each night the people prayed that God would help them get nails and tin to build a roof.

Chico wondered, *Where will we get nails and tin? What good will praying do? Will God make nails and tin rain on us? Oooooh, raining nails might hurt!*

FIVE

The Fight

*

The days went by, but nothing much seemed to happen. The man in the green Jeep had not returned. The church continued to meet in its building with walls, doors, windows, and benches but no roof. It was hot, dry and dusty.

One day at school, in a game of soccer during recess, Chico was running right at the ball when out of the corner of his eye, he saw someone from the other team running at the ball, also. Chico ran harder and kicked at the same time the other player ran close to him. Chico kicked the ball through two rocks on the ground that the players used as goal posts.

"Goooooooooooal!" Suddenly, he was pushed from behind. Thud! Chico hit the ground hard! Calvin was lying on top of him. Chico tried to turn over, but the weight of Calvin on top of him was too much. Calvin growled into Chico's ear, "That will teach you to get in my way." The smells of his raunchy bad breath made breathing difficult! Chico slowly stood up and felt the anger boiling up from his stomach. He shook his head. He was mad! He threw up his fists in the fighting pose. Calvin quickly drew back and hit Chico squarely in the eye.

With his eye stinging and head reeling, Chico couldn't think. He bent over slightly and ran, head-butting Calvin in the stomach. Calvin lunged backward and then stood up. Chico began to swing wildly. Calvin dodged out of the way. Chico was so mad, he was spitting.

He grabbed Calvin around the waist and hugged him while he pounded him in the back. Calvin tripped Chico. Chico held on to Calvin as they fell sideways. Both boys rolled on the ground. Dust flew everywhere. Arms flailed as they slapped and punched as much as two rolling boys could. The soccer game was forgotten. The other players, screaming and yelling, soon were bunched up around Calvin and Chico.

KERSPLASH!! A big bucket of water was thrown on the two boys. Chico and Calvin were so shocked by the water, they stopped fighting and slowly stood up.

Miss Alvarez stood over the now-empty bucket. She grabbed each boy by the ear and dragged him into the school building. Miss Alvarez was a short woman, but she was taking giant steps. Chico was forced to walk fast because of the pain in his ear. The kids crowded around the windows to look inside the school house to see what would happen next. No one made a noise.

"Sit," she commanded. Both boys sat down. The school house was quiet; Chico heard a rooster crow off in the distance. Normally the noise of the children covered the sounds from town.

"Palm up on top of the desk," she directed as she stood in front of Calvin.

Calvin laid his hand out on the desk. Miss Alvarez took a ruler and struck Calvin's palm. Chico flinched. She walloped his hand 10 times. Each time the ruler made a "pop" on Calvin's hand, Chico flinched. Calvin sat looking straight ahead. He didn't say a word or let out a sound.

"Palm up on top of the desk," she demanded of Chico. Chico held out his hand. She slapped the palm of his hand with the ruler. Chico swallowed hard. *I am NOT going to cry!* he told himself. With the second strike, Chico reinforced to himself, *I am NOT going to cry!* With each hit he repeated silently, *I am NOT going to cry!*

"Now both of you go to the chalkboard and write 100 times, 'I will not fight in school.'" Neither boy said a word but marched straight to the chalkboard. The children filed back into the classroom. Chico's hand stung. His eye hurt. It hurt badly! His head pounded. His once-white shirt was muddy and tattered; so were his feelings. He was so ashamed. Mama would be so disappointed. Papa would be so angry.

Chico wrote on the chalkboard, "I will not fight in school." Over and over he wrote. *Bla-thump, bla-thump, bla-thump,* went Chico's eye. *Bla-thump, bla-thump, bla-thump,* went his hand. He barely heard the little kids reciting their math.

"One plus one is two. Two plus one is three. Three plus one is four." And on they recited. *Bla-thump, bla-thump, bla-thump,* went Chico's eye. *Will school never end?*

Bla-thump, Bla-thump, went his hand. All the school children went home. Miss Alvarez sat in the back of the classroom. Calvin and Chico continued to write, "I will not fight in school." They never looked at each other the rest of the day.

The afternoon sun hit the tin roof of the school house. It burned hot in the classroom, as sweat poured into Chico's hurt eye. *Bla-thump, bla-thump, bla-thump,* went Chico's eye. *Bla-thump, bla-thump, bla-thump,* went his hand. *Will I ever finish all the writing?* thought Chico, as he wrote, "I will not fight in school, I will not fight in school, I will not fight in school."

Finally, Miss Alvarez said, "That's enough, boys. Go home." Chico slowly walked home. He knew his sisters had told his Mama what had happened. Chico hurt all over. He could not remember ever feeling this ashamed.

As soon as he entered the house, Mama wrapped her arms around him. Suddenly the whole day of trying not to cry collapsed down on him. His eyes began to leak. Soon his eyes were streams pouring down his cheeks. Mama didn't say a word. She just held him tight. Chico breathed deeply the scent of his mama. Her smell made him feel comfort and love.

Mama said, "Rosa, bring me a bucket of water and a rag." She gently began to wash Chico's face.

"Rosa, go find me some *azotecaballo*, (al-so-TEA-ca-bye-yo), the herb that grows along the edge of the road." Chico could see in his mind the *azotecaballo*, with its dark green, oval-shaped leaves and its tiny, little white flowers in little bunches. *How funny*, thought Chico, *that the herb used for swelling means "the whipped or beaten horse." I sure have been beaten or whipped just like a horse*, he thought. Taking off his shirt Mama washed the rest of him. Chico just stood there and let the cool water wash away all the dirt and hurt feelings. Mama took the leaves from the plant and put them in warm water to sit a while.

Chico took his woven straw mat that was rolled up in the corner of the room. He spread it out next to the wall and lay down. It was too early to go to bed, but Chico didn't care. He just wanted to go to sleep and forget this day. Mama took the leaves and laid them over Chico's eye.

Papa walked in. Chico heard Mama whispering to him and telling him about the fight. Papa chuckled, "Well, I hope he taught the other kid a lesson."

Mama exclaimed, "I don't want any of my children fighting."

Chico heard Papa still chuckling away. *So he isn't angry after all*, thought Chico. Chico dropped off to sleep as he listened to the sounds of his family getting ready to go to the church without a roof.

The next morning was Saturday. Chico was relieved not to have to go back to school and face the rest of the kids. His eye was so swollen, he could barely open it. He climbed the tree behind his house and sat looking out at the world. He remembered climbing the tree with his friend, Marvin, in Porvenir. *Marvin is a nice kid.* Chico remembered all the different things they had talked about. Chico sat in the tree and watched the world go on around him. He felt sore. His eye hurt. He felt dirty and messed up on the inside and the outside. He watched his mama and Rosa walk to the creek to wash clothes. He watched his papa behind the house sharpening his machete with a file. He watched Nanci play with baby Lupe and little Abel in the back doorway. He felt alone and different. He saw Rafael walk up to his house and ask his papa where Chico was.

Chico overheard Papa say, "Don't know where he went. He just left this morning. Maybe he is at the creek with his mama."

"Thanks. How is he feeling after yesterday?" Chico heard Rafael ask.

"Well, his eye is pretty black and swollen. He moves like he is sore."

"Yeah, well, Calvin hit him pretty hard."

"I'm glad he wasn't a coward. I hope he gave that kid what he deserved."

I hope he doesn't tell Papa about me being punished, thought Chico.

Rafael giggled, "He did. Both of them were punished."

"Oh, really! What happened?"

"They got strikes!"

"Humph, strikes."

"Yeah, 10 strikes—the most that Miss Alvarez ever has given anyone!" Chico heard Rafael saying with amazement. "Plus they had to write on the board 100 times, 'I will not fight in school.' She must have been really upset to make them write it so many times."

Papa continued sharpening his machete.

"Well, see ya," said Rafael. He waved over his shoulder as he headed toward the creek.

Chico just sat in the tree and thought, *I might just have to stay up here forever, now that Papa knows I got punished at school.*

Just then Papa leaned his head back against the house and looked up at the tree. He saw Chico!

"Boy! Get down here!" he commanded.

Chico quickly obeyed and climbed down. Chico stood before Papa with his head down.

"Have you been up there all day?"

"Yes," Chico responded weakly.

"You got in trouble yesterday. I will not tolerate your misbehaving in school. I don't want a child of mine getting in trouble and being punished like a little girl. You must be a man! You obviously are not learning to be a man at school. You are going to work with me from now on. I don't want you going back to school."

Chico felt as though his stomach dropped to the ground. No more school. No more learning to read. No more learning math. Spending all day long every day with grouchy old Papa. *My life is over*, thought Chico. Chico ducked his head and trudged into the house.

Late in the afternoon Chico heard a noise off in the distance. It slowly grew louder. It sounded like a truck but not quite. It sounded like the green Jeep but not quite. Several vehicles drove by! Chico could see more clearly now. It was the green Jeep and the dump truck with *Hermano* Larry driving! Both trucks were full of white people. They had all kinds of boxes stacked up on top of the Jeep. In the back of the truck were pieces of tin. The trucks drove up to the roofless church.

A dump truck full of corn getting ready to go to Reitoca

With his head down Chico slowly strolled over to the roofless church. Everyone in all of Reitoca was there. People were shaking each others' hands. Chico hung back to the edge of the crowd. He didn't want anyone to see him. He was embarrassed about his black eye.

These were the strangest-looking people. Some of the men had white hair! Some women with them had yellow-colored hair. All of them had pink, white skin. Some had blue eyes; some had green eyes; some had regular brown eyes. Chico never had seen anything quite like these people. Don Felix tried to get the crowd's attention.

"These are our brothers and sisters in Christ," said Don Felix. He continued, "They're here from the United States to help us finish our church building. Let's thank God that they are here." All the people bowed their heads to pray.

So this is what people from the United States look like, thought Chico. He knew he should bow his head and close his eyes for the prayer, but he just couldn't keep his eyes off one of the men.

He just kept right on staring at the man. He was as big as *Hermano* Larry, but he had red hair. Chico didn't know that people could have red hair. The man also had brown dots all over his white skin.

After the prayer the man looked up and saw Chico staring at him. He smiled a big smile. Chico smiled back with a moan. It was his first smile since the fight. His eye hurt when he smiled.

The man from the green Jeep invited everyone to the big field beside the roofless church later that evening. He was going to show a movie. He explained that a movie was about the life of Jesus. They would show the pictures after dark.

That evening Rafael and all the other boys watched as the man in the green Jeep and several of the Americans tied a big, white sheet to some poles in the middle of the big field. Chico slowly walked up to the other kids.

"Wow, look at your eye!" exclaimed Rafael.

"It is black and blue!" cried out José.

"Can you see out of it?" asked Pedro.

"Just barely," responded Chico.

"Does it hurt?" asked Rafael's little brother.

"Naww," lied Chico. He patted the little kid's head and tried to pretend he was okay.

Just then the people began to sing.

"Let's sit up front on the grass," said José.

"Sure," responded Chico. He felt good being back with his friends.

"I see the man in the green Jeep," pointed Pedro, "Let's go see what he is doing."

The boys took off at a trot to see the man in the green Jeep. The man from the green Jeep started up a little blue machine that sat behind the green Jeep.

"What's that thing?" asked José.

"It's a generator," said the man in the green Jeep as he laid down a yellow-colored line to another machine sitting on a table closer to the white sheet.

"This is a projector," the man in the Jeep said. "And this is the picture." He pointed to a big, round thing. "Look right here. You can see tiny pictures. The projector will shine a light though them and make them be big on the screen up there," he said as he pointed to the sheet. "The project will move the pictures so fast that they will look like real people. Now, run up front and sit down; we'll get started."

They sang along with all the people. "Praise the Lord, Praise the Lord," sang the crowd that was gathering. Chico looked around. He guessed everyone in all of Reitoca was there. Chico clapped but didn't sing. Singing hurt his eye!

The moving pictures started! Chico never had seen anything quite like this! These were the same stories he had heard from the little church without a roof. Jesus was born as a little baby in a cow pen. He grew up and began to teach the people. Jesus and the disciples went fishing. While they were in the boat, they found themselves in a storm—as big as the one that knocked down the corn there in Reitoca. Jesus stood up and stopped the storm! It was incredible. Wow! What a wonderful story!

That night, lying on his straw mat, Chico could see in his mind all the different pictures. The poor, blind man that

Jesus made see again; the little girl who was dead and returned to life when Jesus told her to get up. All he had to do was remember. In his mind he could see it all over again.

Monday morning Chico went with his papa to work at the church with all the Americans. The big, brown-spotted, red-haired man was there.

The big man walked over to Chico and pointed at himself. He said, "Raymond." Chico understood his name was Raymond.

So Chico pointed at himself and said, "Chico." The big, brown-spotted, red-haired man stuck out his hand. Chico offered his hand in return. The man's hand swallowed up Chico's small, brown one as they shook hands.

The big man pointed at Chico's eye. "Ouch!" he said.

Chico nodded his head up and down. "Ouch!" he echoed back.

The big man said a bunch of words. Chico didn't understand him, but he did understand his smile. He knew the red-haired man wanted Chico to help him. Chico looked up at his papa to see if that would be okay. Papa nodded. So Chico went with the big, brown-spotted, red-haired man. The man had a ruler that wound up inside a little yellow box that he clipped on his belt.

Chico held the ruler in the place where Raymond showed him. Raymond took a big, flat pencil out of his pocket and marked on the wood. Raymond took a big, round-looking machine that made a big huge roar and sat it on the wood at the mark. The machine ate the wood into two pieces! Unbelievable!

The big, red-haired man and Chico worked together all morning long. At noon they sat together under the tree. Some of the women from the church brought them plates of food. The white ladies came around with glasses of pink, sweet drink. Chico grinned at the big, red-haired man. The man grinned back.

Each night the people met together in the field behind the church. The man in the green Jeep showed more pictures of Jesus. Each night one of the Americans talked in his or her funny way that only that the Americans understood. They told what Jesus meant to them.

The man from the green Jeep told the crowd what the Americans said. Each day Chico worked with his new friend, Raymond.

One day Raymond gave Chico some gum to chew. It was pink and tasted so very good. Raymond showed how to flatten the gum in his mouth, stick his tongue into it, and then blow air into the gum. Raymond blew a little bubble. Chico tried it. He carefully flattened the gum with his tongue and then blew air. His gum flew straight out of his mouth and landed on Raymond's pants leg. Chico looked up in horror. Raymond laughed the loudest laugh Chico had ever heard.

Raymond gave Chico a new piece of gum. This time Chico very carefully held the gum in his mouth as he slowly blew a nice, pink bubble. Raymond and Chico laughed and worked together every day.

The men took all the wood that Chico and Raymond had cut and nailed it together. On Wednesday they put these big wooden things on top of the walls of the church. Then men climbed up on top of it and nailed down the tin pieces that the Americans had brought in the truck. By Thursday their little church had a roof! A nice, shinny tin roof! Chico had helped!

At the end of the week Raymond gave Chico his blue ball cap. It was too big for Chico, but he wore it proudly. Every time he wore this blue ball cap, he always would remember Raymond.

The last night of the pictures some horrible men killed Jesus. They took him to a judge. The judge ordered Jesus' death. They nailed Jesus to a big, wooden cross. Chico felt sick watching what those cruel people did. Some of the women watching the film were crying. The women in the film went to the cave where they had put Jesus' body. He was not there. He was alive! He wasn't like a ghost walking around. It really was Jesus. It wasn't spooky, either. After Jesus spoke to His disciples, He went up into heaven.

At the end of the picture the man from the green Jeep asked if anyone wanted to stand by him and pray to God. Chico saw his sister, Rosa; Rafael's sister, Virginia; Chema, Virginia's friend; and many other people go to the front and kneel down. Chico looked around for his papa but didn't see him.

The next morning all the Americans packed their stuff back into the boxes and put the boxes back on the top of the green Jeep. Raymond had a little camera and took pictures. Each time he took a picture, a small piece of white paper popped out of the front of his camera. It would slowly start turning colors. Soon you could see the pictures. Raymond motioned for Chico to stand by him. He handed the camera to another American. Raymond stood up with his arm around Chico. *Click* went the camera; slowly a piece of white paper popped out of the camera. Raymond squatted down next to Chico. They watched. Slowly colors appeared. There on the paper was a picture of Raymond and Chico. Raymond handed the picture to Chico. He spoke some more funny words and gave Chico a big hug. Raymond got into the back of the truck.

Chico stood in the road and waved as his friend, Raymond, drove off in the dust. Running home Chico showed his mother the picture of Raymond and himself.

70

"It's beautiful!" she exclaimed. "Let's stick it up on the back of the door."

She took the old string of garlic down and threw it in the fire. She put a tiny hole in the top of the picture and hung it on the nail that had held the garlic up. The door sure looked different! Chico had never seen the door without the garlic on it. Would the evil spirits get upset with them for taking down the garlic? Chico didn't care. He had a picture of a special friend hanging on the back of the door.

Papa walked though the door and sniffed the air.

"What is that smell?" he asked

"It's the garlic Mama threw in the fire," responded Nanci.

"What on earth?" he bellowed. "What will protect us from the evil spirits?"

"God will protect us," responded Mama in her quiet, loving voice.

Papa wrinkled up his forehead and shook his head, but he didn't say another word.

That evening as Chico and Rafael sat outside under the stars talking, they noticed someone walking down the road carrying firewood. "Look," Rafael whispered. "Someone is carrying firewood."

"It's too late at night for him to be working," said Chico.

"It is someone leaving firewood to ask a girl to marry him!" responded Rafael.

"Let's follow him and see who he is asking to marry him!"

"Shh, he will hear you. Let's follow! Run to that bush over there."

The boys crept along behind. Soon they realized they were almost to Rafael's house. It must be Chema. He wanted to see whether Virginia really loved him. As Chema got closer to the house, he took a bucket of water that he had left there earlier and poured the water over the wood.

"Why is he pouring water over the wood?" whispered Chico.

"If she burns his offering of wood, that means she will marry him. If she throws it out, that means she doesn't want him," answered Rafael. "If it's wet, she really will have to work to show that she wants to marry him."

Rafael and Chico began to giggle and scampered off back to Chico's house. Would Virginia burn the firewood and get married? Or would she throw it out?

SIX

The Wedding

*

The next morning as soon as Chico could get away, he ran to Rafael's house. Smoke was emerging from the kitchen cook fire. Chico went around to the back door by the kitchen and found Virginia vigorously fanning the cook fire.

"Why are you using wet wood?" quizzed Chico.

Virginia didn't reply. She just muttered under her breath, "I'll get a good fire going out of this wood, if I have to spend all day doing it!"

Rafael grabbed Chico's arm as he ran out the door. Both boys collapsed in laughter outside.

"Looks like we are going to have a wedding," sing-songed Rafael.

"Oh, they are in love," laughed Chico as he wiggled his eyebrows up.

"Yeah, kissy kissy," giggled back Rafael.

A few days latter Chema and Virginia nailed a paper to the big tree in the center of town. The paper stated that they were to be married. If anyone didn't think they should get married, that person was to go to the *Cacique* (ka-SEE-key), who was the leader in town, and tell him. Of course, no one did.

A week later Virginia and Chema walked over to the big town and wrote their names in the big registry book where the government man keeps all the official records. On the walk back they talked about their wedding plans. Of course, everyone would be invited. Chema's papa had a pig that they would kill and roast. Virginia's mama had several chickens they could cook. Virginia had a cousin that had a really pretty white dress she would loan Virginia. Chema had been making adobe blocks. They would add a room to Virginia's mother's house and live there. Life together would be wonderful.

Everyone in town got excited about the big celebration. Don Felix went into the big town and took his two donkeys loaded up with bags of beans to sell. The money he made off the sale of beans he would use to buy sugar, salt, and paper for decorations for the wedding celebration. José's mama had a big oven where she could bake a cake.

Chico helped Rafael sweep the dirt around the house. They packed it down tightly so it would have no dust. Burning leaves and trash was fun for Rafael and Chico. Some of the older boys in town whitewashed the wall of the house. Chico and Rafael were sent out to find different-colored clay out of the mountainside. The older girls used the colored clays to paint flowers on the fresh, white walls. The boys hunted firewood until they had a huge stack. They also gathered pine needles from high in the mountains. The pine needles were to be sprinkled on the church floor for the day. The boys tormented and irritated the older girls, who made baskets of white paper flowers. The boys went from house to house asking to borrow people's tables and chairs. They helped the men set up tables and chairs in the yard.

The day before the big day, family members from neighboring towns arrived. Even the man in the green Jeep and his wife arrived! Smiling people were slapping each other on the backs and shaking each others' hands. People were everywhere in the large house. Some sat in the big patio and visited. Some stood around Rafael's old Uncle Pepe and sang as he played the guitar under the almond tree in the center of the patio. The women congregated around the food preparations in the big kitchen on one end of the adobe house. Big pots of sweet coffee filled the evening air with a sweet, tangy fragrance.

Chico and Rafael wandered from group to group. In one group people were telling old stories about the time when they were children. One group was talking about planting corn and arguing about when the moon would be in the right position so the corn would grow better. The women just talked about women-stuff like babies and whose daughter would be next to get married. Chico and Rafael didn't stay listening to the women very long.

The men were telling the story about when Rafael's papa fell out of a tree. He fell on a chicken! The poor, angry chicken had squawked and tried to run off, but its leg was broken. They killed the poor, crippled chicken and cooked it. Rafael's papa had to eat the broken leg. However, the chicken got its revenge. Ever since then Rafael's papa had walked with a limp! Rafael's papa tried to tell them he had hurt his ankle when he fell, but no one heard him above the laughter.

Chico heard a familiar voice talking about how long they had taken to walk over! Chico knew that voice. He turned around. He saw Marvin with all his family!

"Marvin!" he called out.

"Hey, Chico!" grinned Marvin. He grabbed Chico's outstretched hand.

"Why are you here?" Chico asked, as he pumped Marvin's hand up and down.

"Chema is my cousin!" responded Marvin, as he continued to shake Chico's hand enthusiastically .

"Glad you are here. This is my friend Rafael," introduced Chico, as he dropped Marvin's hand.

"Ahh, Rafael, I have heard about you." He lightly punched Rafael in the arm.

"Rafael, Rafael," called Rafael's mama.

"Over here," he answered from the dark shadows.

"Boys, will you take these matches and go around and light all the lanterns? Please," she asked.

"Sure," the three boys chorused together. Laughing at themselves, they took the matches.

In each room a small can sat on the shelf. These were the brake-fluid cans from the big trucks that drove through town. The truck drivers threw the cans out on the side of the road when the cans were empty. The cans made great lanterns. A slit had been cut in the lid; a tightly woven wick went into the can and up through the lid's slit. Then the cans were filled with kerosene. The boys lit each wick. The little lanterns gave a warm, yellow glow to each room. People sat around the rooms and talked. As the evening grew, some people began to doze off in their chairs. Others continued to visit quietly. Not too many people planned on sleeping. They were too excited to see each other.

Someone else showed up with another guitar. Then someone showed up with a big, fat guitar called a *guittarón*. Music was played all night long.

Late in the night the man in the green Jeep and his wife were so sleepy, they finally spread out a little mat and lay down on the floor in the middle of one of the rooms and slept. People all around watched and continued their conversations. Very late in the night the three boys spread out mats beside the man from the green Jeep and went to sleep, also.

The next morning everyone was given tortillas with refried beans and big chunks of white cheese. They washed the food down with sweet coffee with the special treat of milk added. The boys took off for a bath at the creek. Everyone seemed to be down at the creek, too. Even the bride, Virginia, and all her friends were there. Very carefully one of her girlfriends was combing out and braiding Virginia's hair into one long braid down her back, so when it dried, it would be wavy. The boys really couldn't splash and play like they would normally. Too many adults that didn't want to be splashed were there.

Boys on the side of the creek prepare for their baths.

Once back at the house Virginia and her mother got on their horse and rode off to Virginia's grandmother's house. You could see the house off in the distance. *Did she change her mind?* thought Chico, *Did her mama not want her to marry Chema? Were they hiding out at Virginia's grandmother's?*

Now all dressed up in their best clothes, people continued to visit. Virginia's friends went to the little church and hung up all the paper flowers and sprinkled pine needles on the floor. The little church looked beautiful.

At about noon, Chema, all dressed up in a blue, long-sleeved shirt and new blue jeans and new cowboy hat, jumped on his horse. All of his friends were dressed very much like Chema. They got on their horses, also. Chico, Rafael, Marvin, and José stood together watching them.

"Yip, Yip, Yip," they all hollered while slapping the backside of their horses with their hats. The horses shot out of the yard as if they were scared to death. Everyone stood along beside the fence where the horses had been tied up. They watched the young men hoot and holler and ride like the wind across the hill toward Virginia's grandmother's.

Virginia walked out dressed in blue jeans and a bright red shirt. Chema grabbed her up on his horse. In a flash they were riding back toward the house. The ride back didn't take long. The triumphant cowboy brought back his bride-to-be with yipping, clomping of horses' hooves, and dust flying everywhere! Virginia's mother arrived riding at the rear with one of the other boys. Everyone cheered and welcomed Chema. They slapped him on the back and laughed.

Virginia and her friends slipped back inside the house. They helped her get dressed in the beautiful white dress. The difficult part was helping her put on the pretty, white shoes that someone let her borrow. The shoes were really too small; Virginia had not worn shoes much in her life. The woman from the green Jeep sprinkled white powder in the shoes. That helped Virginia finally get her feet inside the shoes, but the fit was very tight.

Everyone gathered inside the church building. The guitars and *guittarón* players stood at the front of the church. They all had found yellow shirts and black pants, so they all looked alike, except the shirt that the *guittarón* player wore wouldn't button all the way down over his little, fat tummy. He didn't seem to mind; he would just hold the fat *guittarón* in front of him. No one would notice that his shirt wasn't buttoned.

The church smelled like the sweet, green smell of pine needles. Paper white flowers were stuck on the side walls and on the end of each bench. The man from the green Jeep stood in front of two chairs that had been decorated in white paper. Paper flowers were placed down front. Chema, grinning like he was so smart, stood beside the man from the green Jeep.

The music started. The people tapped their toes and enjoyed the music, but where was the bride? What was taking her so long? The music continued to play. Some people started singing along with the music.

Chema kept looking toward the back door of the church. Wiping his sweaty hands on his pants Chema turned and looked out the window toward Virginia's house. *Where was she?*

Finally, out the window Chico saw Virginia walking over with her mother and her friends. Everyone heard Chema let out a deep breath. Virginia's black, shiny hair fell in beautiful waves all down her back and over the sparkling, white dress. Two by two, Chema's and Virginia's friends paired off. The couples lined the aisle of the church. Virginia slowly walked up the aisle. She was wearing no shoes! You could still see the white powder on her brown feet, but she had no shoes! Chico snickered. Rafael whispered, "Her feet were too fat for the shoes." Marvin's mother tapped the boys on the shoulder. "Shh," she whispered.

Virginia walked up to Chema and took his hand. They sat down together in the special chairs. All of Virginia and Chema's friends sat on the benches that had been waiting for them at the front.

The man in the green Jeep told a story, "Ten young women were waiting on their bridegroom. Some were prepared and some were not. They all brought lanterns with them, but five had brought along extra oil. The other five had not. The bridegroom was late arriving. Not the bride!" Everyone giggled. Virginia ducked her head.

The man in the green Jeep continued, "So they all lit their lanterns while they were waiting. Just like last night at Virginia's the lanterns were lit as we waited on this special day. Some of the girls fell asleep—just like last night, some of us fell asleep. When they heard the bridegroom arrive, they trimmed the wicks in their lanterns and got ready to welcome him. The unprepared, foolish girls said to the wise, prepared girls, 'Give us some of your oil, so that we can welcome the bridegroom.' 'No,' they responded, 'There will not be enough oil for both of us. Quickly go buy oil.' So the foolish, unprepared girls went to buy oil. While they were gone, the bridegroom came. The wise, prepared girls went with him. The door was closed. When the foolish, unprepared girls returned from buying oil, they knocked and pounded on the door, yelling, 'Please let us in.' But the bridegroom replied, 'I don't know you.'"

"Ahh, how sad," said a little girl.

Her mother said, "Shh."

The man from the green Jeep said, "You are right. It is sad. These girls knew they should be ready for the bridegroom. He didn't ride up on a horse to take them away, but he did arrive. Some were ready; others weren't.

"Jesus is the bridegroom. We are His brides. We must be ready for the day when He arrives for us. Virginia and

Chema have taken a step of faith to trust Jesus. They want to be ready for when the Lord arrives. What a beautiful way to start their lives together, with Jesus as the head of their home!"

Five smart, prepared girls and five, foolish girls, thought Chico. He remembered the night he had spent up in the mountains on his way to his Aunt Sara's house. He hadn't taken a lantern or oil—not even matches to light a fire. He was not a smart, prepared person. Marvin, on the return trip, had matches and had started a fire. He was smart and was prepared.

Chema and Virginia stood up and promised to love each other forever and to love God forever. The man in the green Jeep told them they could kiss each other. Chema quickly gave her a little peck on the cheek.

"No, that's not what I meant by a kiss. You can do better than that," challenged the man in the green Jeep. Everyone laughed.

Red color slowly crept up Chema's neck to his cheeks. Virginia instantly turned rosy red. Giggling, Rafael punched Chico with his elbow. Giggling, Chico punched giggling Marvin. Chema leaded over and kissed Virginia on the lips. Clapping and laughing the people watched Chema and Virginia smile and run out of the church building.

Rapidly everyone followed them back to Virginia's house. The afternoon was filled with good food, laughter, guitar-playing and singing. The day passed quickly. Soon time arrived for them to go home. Chico lay on his straw mat. He felt full of good food and good friends. Tomorrow, Sunday, was to be a special day also.

Chico awoke and lay on his mat with his eyes closed. He heard a rooster crowing off in the distance. He heard Don Felix's donkeys braying. He heard his papa say to his mama, "I just don't understand why you have to do this."

"I must do this to show everyone that Jesus has changed me," she softly replied.

"Why do you believe you have to change? What was wrong with the way we were before? You prayed to the Virgin Mary and the saints. We hung garlic on the door and went to the *curandero* (cu-ran-DARE-row) when we were sick."

"I've told you. Jesus has forgiven me and lives within me. The saints never did that for me. Besides now I can pray straight to God. I don't need the saints to pray for me."

"All right, but I think you were just fine before all this Jesus talk started," concluded Papa.

The next morning everyone gathered at the church. Don Felix explained that since the man in the green Jeep was with them as well as all the families visiting for the wedding, they would be celebrating baptism.

"Let us walk down to the creek," invited Don Felix. So many people were gathered, they wouldn't all fit inside the little church anyway. Standing on the creek bank under the shade, the guitar players started singing about Jesus. Everyone joined in.

Some of the boys climbed the trees around the creek. Rafael and Marvin talked the whole way to the creek. Chico had followed along behind. He felt a little left out. He wanted his two best friends to be friends, but they seemed to have more in common with each other than either one of them had with him. Rafael and Marvin sat together on a tree limb and sang all the songs with robust enthusiasm. Chico sat on a lower branch of the tree and watched them.

The man from the green Jeep walked into the creek water and asked those that were to be baptized to make a line along the creek shore. Standing along the shore were his mama, Rosa, José, Chema, Virginia, Don Felix, his wife, Miss Alvarez, and Rafael's mama and papa. Rafael was climbing down out of the tree to stand along the shore. Chico thought, *Papa and I are going to be the only real men left in town.* Chico looked over at where his papa stood in the back of the crowd. Papa's face looked stern. Chico knew Papa was not happy.

The man in the green Jeep took each person and asked him or her whether he or she had trusted Jesus as Savior. Then he lowered them, one by one, into the water, as he said, "I baptize you in the name of the Father, Son, and Holy Spirit." The crowd on the creek bank sang a song about baptism. Chico sat fascinated. Chico felt as though his heart was beating faster. He felt a funny, quivery feeling in his stomach. More people were walking out into the water to be baptized when Chico slowly climbed down the tree.

The green Jeep visits Reitoca.

SEVEN

Rosa's Trees

*

Chico felt really weird. He walked over to where his papa stood. Papa laid his hand on Chico's shoulder. Chico could see the angry glaze in Papa's eye.

"Remember, Chico. We are men. We don't need God," he said. Chico nodded in agreement without really understanding.

After the baptism, all the kids ran down and jumped into the water. Chico just stood there with his papa's hand on his shoulder. He really wanted to jump in the water. He felt strange to be standing there with Papa, yet he didn't want to let the moment go.

Finally Papa turned and began walking up the bank back to town.

"Hey, Chico. Get in the water with us," Marvin called to him.

"Yeah, get in," echoed Rafael.

Ignoring his friends Chico stood there while the older people walked by him. He heard snatches of conversations.

People were saying, "Congratulations on trusting Christ." "I'm so happy for you."

The baptized people were responding, "God has been so good to me." "It is such a relief to be forgiven." "Now our whole family is serving the Lord." "I feel like a burden has been taken off of me." "I feel so clean."

Humph, thought Chico. *How can you be clean when you weren't in the water very long and didn't even use soap?*

"Chico, Chico," interrupted Rafael and Marvin.

Chico walked toward the creek. He took off his pants, shoes, and shirt and threw them into the grass with all the other boys' clothes. *Kersplash,* went Chico as he jumped in. As soon as his head popped up, Rafael dunked him down again. Then Chico went under the water and pulled Rafael's feet out from under him. *Splash*, Rafael went as he fell backward into the water. Marvin dunked Rafael as soon as he emerged. On it went. The water felt cool. The boys laughed and played. The whole time Chico still felt that quivery feeling in his tummy.

The next morning, Marvin and his family were leaving. Rafael and Chico arrived to say good-bye.

"I will pray for you," he told Chico.

Chico said, "Uh, okay," and looked at his feet.

Rafael and Marvin hugged. "See ya, brother," they said to each other. Chico felt left out. "Uh, see ya," Chico said.

Miss Alvarez had said that so much had happened, they would wait and start school back the next day. So Rafael and Chico had a whole day to do nothing. They went to the creek for a while and then sat in the shade a while. At night they watched the stars. It was a nice, nothing day.

That nice, nothing day ended even nicer. Mama talked to Papa. They decided to let Chico go back to school.

But Papa said, "Only if he can promise me that he will not get into trouble."

So Chico returned to school. The regular routine of the same thing every day was calming. The school days all seemed to flow from one to another. Nothing much seemed to happen. Calvin was still there, but Chico tried to avoid him. Calvin seemed to avoid Chico, so things went smoothly. Every day Chico wore his cap, which his American friend, Raymond, had given him. Chico wished Raymond would return to Reitoca. He had so much fun working with Raymond.

Miss Alvarez left the classroom one day as she said, "Put your papers on my desk. When you are finished, you may leave."

Chico was not paying attention to the others in the classroom. He was just trying to remember what six times eight was.

Someone walked by on the way to the teacher's desk. Then suddenly Chico saw his cap ripped off the front of his desk. He grabbed for it and looked up.

There Calvin stood grinning, saying, "I need a new cap." Putting the cap on, Calvin quickly stalked to the door. Chico started after him. Rafael grabbed Chico and threw him back in his chair.

"Don't!" he warned as Miss Alvarez walked in.

"Is everything okay in here?"

"Yes, Miss Alvarez," responded Rafael as he sat back down in his own chair.

"What are you doing out of your chair?" demanded Miss Alvarez.

"Nothing."

"Was Chico involved in this?"

"No, Miss Alvarez. I was bothering him."

"I'm surprised at you. You usually are a good boy."

"Bring me your paper," she commanded. Rafael didn't say anything. He slowly walked up to the front.

"Palm up on the desk," she demanded.

Chico cringed inside as Rafael stuck out his hand. Miss Alvarez struck his hand two times and told him to sit down. Rubbing his hand, Rafael passed Chico. He smiled and whispered, "It's okay."

Chico's face was burning. *That was my cap that Raymond gave me. My friend Raymond.* Chico finally turned his paper in. He never did remember what six times eight was. He left it blank along with about five other problems.

As he walked out the door, Rafael grabbed him and said, "Leave it alone! He is not worth getting in trouble for. He is worse than cow manure! He just doesn't know how to be nice. You do, so just leave him alone."

"I just hate him. I hate him," sputtered out Chico. "He stole my cap and caused you to get strikes." Chico balled up his fists.

"I know, I know," sympathized Rafael, "but it is not worth fighting about." José, Pedro, and some of the other boys joined the group and echoed what Rafael was saying about Calvin.

Chico was so angry, he didn't know what to say. He finally just nodded his head up and down. Finally he put his balled-up fists in his pockets. What else could he do with so many people around telling him not to fight?

Walking home Chico realized that Rafael had taken the strikes that he should have gotten. Chico—not Rafael—was the one angry. Rafael was a true friend! He had been trying to stop Chico from getting in another fight and into more trouble.

A week later, Rosa arrived at home limping, with tears running down her face. "Mama!" she called loudly.

"She is over at José's mama's for a Bible study," said Chico. "What's wrong?"

"I fell and hurt my ankle," she cried as she slumped into the chair.

"What happened?"

"We were running and playing chase when I stepped into a hole and fell. My ankle really hurts."

"It is swelling," sympathized Chico. "I can go get some *azotecaballo* leaves, if you want me to," he offered.

"That would be nice, but before you go, will you get me a drink of water and wrap a cool, wet rag over my ankle, please?"

When Mama returned later and found Rosa in the hammock with *azotecaballo* leaves on her ankle and Chico sitting on the ground beside her to keep her company, she was amazed.

"You children have grown up so much. I am so proud of you," Mama said.

The following afternoon after school, Mama said, "Chico, since Rosa can't walk, I need you to go out and gather firewood for me. I know that girls usually gather firewood, but Rosa can't go." Chico looked shocked. *Doing woman's work!* he thought.

"Take Nanci with you," she added.

Nanci's little, short legs made the job longer. Finding firewood took all afternoon. Nanci sat down on a big rock.

"I can't walk anymore," she said.

Chico thought, *She is just a little kid.* For the next five days Chico and Nanci went every day to search for firewood. It was hot, tiring, and boring work. Chico realized that this "woman's work" was not very easy. A lot of firewood was needed to keep a fire going to cook all the food for their large family. Rosa had said this was her least-favorite chore. Now Chico understood why. She much preferred to help with the cooking—anything but gathering firewood. Chico remembered his grandmother telling stories about when she was a girl in Reitoca. With shade trees everywhere things had been cooler. Firewood was just a short walk from the house.

The next week Mama was braiding Rosa's long, black hair. "Rosa, quit wiggling," warned Mama. Chico watched his sister wiggle. She was excited because today the man from the green Jeep was having a special meeting at the church.

"Chico, I want you to go with us." Chico groaned inwardly. He and Papa had not gone back to the church meetings since Mama and Rosa had been baptized. They agreed they didn't need Jesus. They were strong men and didn't need anybody. At least he and Papa had one thing they agreed on.

"I need your help today," Chico heard his Mama say.

Rosa and her mother walked down the dirt road to the church. Chico followed along behind. Rosa skipped and ran ahead. *Her ankle sure is lots better,* thought Chico. *I think she has been faking it because she didn't want to go out and gather the firewood.* The day was hot. Chico wished more shade trees were along the way, like Grandmother had talked about.

The people inside the little church already were singing. Chico, Rosa, and Mama quickly found a place to sit. It was cool inside the dirt-floored, adobe church. The cool felt nice after the long walk. Smiling, Rosa began to sing as she wiped the sweat off her forehead. Chico felt that quivering feeling in his tummy again. He hadn't had that feeling since the baptism.

Rosa listened to the man from the green Jeep speaking about how God created the earth and told Adam and Eve to take care of it. Chico listened but, by looking out the window, pretended not to. Chico was amazed that God created all the earth, the animals, the water, the trees, and all the plants. God had commanded people to take care of His wonderful creation. If people took care of the earth, they would have plenty to eat and firewood to use for cooking. Chico listened as people in the church talked about how they also were responsible for taking care for the earth. One way they could care for the earth was to plant more trees.

Rosa sat up straight and listened carefully as the women all talked about how far they had to go to bring firewood home each day. Since he had to search for the firewood, Chico understood how far the trip was. Rosa surely was agreeing with them! Chico rubbed his neck and shoulder. His neck certainly was tired from carrying the firewood.

The man from the green Jeep told them of a type of tree called a Lucerne tree. It was the fastest-growing tree in the world. The families could plant the trees near their houses. By planting trees they would be obeying God by caring for the earth.

Wow! thought Chico, *We would not have to walk so far to get firewood.* The man from the green Jeep gave Rosa, Chico, and Mama each an armful of trees growing in black plastic bags. The walk home was difficult with all the black bags of trees, but Rosa didn't mind. She couldn't wait to see her trees grow big. Chico trudged along behind and tried not to drop a bag.

Eagerly Rosa helped her mother dig the holes to plant the trees. She carefully patted the dirt down around each tree. The little trees barely touched her knees.

"You really think these will be big trees one day? Ha! They never will be big enough for firewood," mocked Chico.

"Yes, they will," snapped Rosa.

Every day Rosa carefully watered each tree. "Grow, grow, grow," she would whisper to each tree as she gave it water. A month later the trees were as tall as Rosa.

As Rosa carried the firewood each day, Chico heard her pray, "Oh, God, help our little trees to grow." A few months later the trees were as tall as Rosa's mother.

One hot day Papa called Chico. "Bring the machete. Cut off the bottom branch of each one of these trees," he told Chico.

Smiling, Rosa skipped around and gathered the cut branches to use for firewood.

Rosa seemed to talk all the time about how they were responsible for caring for the earth. Chico realized that with all the trees around the house, the house was much cooler.

One evening as Chico started into the house, he heard his papa roaring in anger. Chico stopped. He didn't want to go in if Papa was in that kind of mood. He listened closely to find out what was going on. Chico heard Papa say, "I'm not good enough for you now. You want me to go to church and be like you. You're a woman. I'm a man. I don't need God."

"We all need God," Mama responded in her quiet, calm voice. "I just want you to walk with me and be there with me. I'm not asking you to change unless you want to. I will always love you and care for you. Just walk with me," she pleaded.

"I will walk you over, but I'll stand outside," Papa said, a little more softly.

"That would be nice. Chico needs to be there, too."

"Oh, all right," he conceded. "We'll go."

That night Chico and Papa stood outside the side window of the church. Chico saw Rafael and his family enter. Calvin, wearing Raymond's blue cap turned backward on his head, stood outside the back door with his papa.

Chico's tummy quivered as the people sang and prayed. Everyone had started calling Don Felix "Brother Felix." Chico didn't listen much as Brother Felix preached. Brother

Felix asked if anyone wanted to pray and trust Jesus. Calvin's papa stepped into the lantern light from the back door. He walked forward and knelt down to pray.

Chico's mouth hung open. Calvin's papa was the meanest man in town. Chico stared at the man kneeling down with a hole in the sole of his boot. Suddenly Calvin appeared beside him and knelt down beside his papa. In his hand he held the cap Raymond had given Chico.

After the closing prayer, Chico continued to watch from the side window. Everyone was hugging Calvin and his father. The men were slapping him on his back and laughing. Rafael even went up and hugged Calvin.

How can he hug Calvin? Doesn't Rafael remember that Calvin is our enemy? Chico thought.

The next day at school, Calvin walked up to Chico. "Here is your cap back. Sorry." Calvin laid the cap in Chico's lap. Chico's mouth dropped open. No words emerged. He turned to look at Rafael, who grinned at Chico.

Chico thought, *This is some kind of trick. After school he will try to steal it back.*

Miss Alvarez said, "Tomorrow we will have a work day. Everyone—bring your rakes, shovels, brooms, and anything else we might need. We will clean the schoolhouse and school yard." She continued, "Bring any flowers or pretty plants we could plant here at the school."

After school the boys decided to go looking for ripe mangos. The sweet, orange mangos with a thin skin were stringy, but sucking the sweet juice out of them was the best-tasting thing around. The boys climbed the big mango tree outside of town as Chico asked Rafael, "Do you think Calvin meant it when he gave me back my cap?"

"He gave you back the cap, didn't he?" responded Rafael. Chico thought, *Hating someone is difficult when he does something nice to you.*

"Look! Brother Felix's donkeys," said Rafael as he pointed below them. One of Don Felix's donkeys was right under the low branch of the tree. It was nibbling a fallen mango.

"Let's jump on its back and take a ride," said Chico.

"On the count of three, grab my back. We will jump."

"One, two, three," they counted together.

With a flying leap they jumped together and landed on the back of the unsuspecting donkey. The poor animal let out a loud, *"Haaaeeeeee."* The four-legged beast took off as fast as his short legs could run. The boys held on to the animal's neck while they wrapped their legs around its middle. With a speed the boys didn't know a donkey had, the creature took off across the hillside. The poor donkey was bellowing; the boys were screaming.

EIGHT

The Paved Road

*

Chico held on tightly to the donkey's neck. Rafael held on tightly to Chico. The donkey ran crazily about. The animal kicked up his back legs and let out a screech. He threw the boys into his neck, where Chico got a better hold of the donkey. The creature turned and ran back to the mango tree. The boys were headed for the low branch.

"Duck!" screamed Rafael. Too late! *Craaack*, sounded Chico's head against the low branch. *Wa-lump, wa-lump!* The branch raked both boys off and dumped them on the hard ground. A huge bump instantly appeared on Chico's forehead. He was lying on top of Rafael. Chico rolled over.

Rafael stood, "What a ride!" he screamed.

Chico lay on the ground. He laughed and cried in pain at the same time. "Oh, my head!"

Rafael wiped the laughing tears from his eyes. "You got quite a goose egg!"

Chico shook his head and slowly sat up, still laughing, as he saw the donkey running off in the distance.

The walk home with the big bump on his forehead seemed long. Every time he and Rafael thought of their wild ride, they broke into giggles and then into laughter. Yes, they would be sore from falling off the donkey on the hard ground. They would have a few bruises, but the bruises were worth the wild, exhilarating ride.

The next day Chico and his sisters gathered several of the family's tools. Chico started to take Raymond's cap and put it on his head. Then he thought, "No, I'd better leave it here. Calvin might just steal it again!"

He placed it back on the kitchen table as he went through the door. Rosa had several trees that she had started growing in plastic bags. She was going to plant them at the school. She still was really big on taking care of the earth. She said, "It's my Christian duty!" Chico rolled his eyes at her. As they walked down the road, a big, blue magpie jaybird flew by.

"Look," pointed Rosa. "Isn't it beautiful with its white throat and blue back?"

"I like its little curly thing sticking out of its head."

"Raah, Raah, Raah," loudly called the blue, spectacular creature.

Up from behind came running Nanci. "Here," she shoved Raymond's cap into Chico's hand. "You forgot it; I knew you would want it."

"Uh, thanks," he said and put it on his head. He would just have to protect his head all day long. The cap did cover the black and blue bump on his forehead.

Miss Alvarez made several assignments of work to be done. She assigned Chico to rake and clean up outside. Chico began looking around for Calvin. Miss Alvarez had assigned Calvin to pull up buckets of water from the well. *That won't keep him busy enough*, thought Chico. *I will just have to be on the lookout for him.*

As Chico raked, dust blew up. This made seeing Calvin more difficult as he walked up from behind Chico.

"Let me sprinkle some water over this area to keep the dust down," said Calvin.

Chico put one hand on his cap on top of his head. Chico didn't know what to say, so he said nothing.

After a while he had a pile of old papers, leaves, and other trash in a pile. Chico squatted over to pick up the trash. He scooped it up with both hands. Calvin ran up. Chico flinched and started dropping the trash.

"Let me help you," eagerly said Calvin as he scooped up the trash.

They carried it over to a barrel and dropped it in. Calvin went back for more trash. Chico, with one hand on his cap, stood there watching Calvin.

"Why are you helping me?" asked Chico when Calvin returned.

"I want to."

"You have never wanted to in the past," stated Chico.

"Yeah, but now I am a whole new kid," grinned Calvin.

Impossible! thought Chico. *He sure is making hating him tough.*

* * * * *

"Chico," called Mama, "I need you to take this bucket and search for horse manure. I need this bucket filled."

"What?" asked Chico with big eyes.

"Horse manure. I need a bucket full," Mama said.

"Whatever for?"

"We ladies are going to build new stoves that will use less fire wood. The man in the green Jeep has brought someone to teach us how to do it. The men have gotten us sand and mud, but each lady is to bring a bucket of horse manure and a bucket of chopped-up straw. Bring it to me by mid-morning to the side yard of the church building," she said.

"You are going to make stoves out of straw, sand, mud, and horse manure?"

"Yes, we are going to mix it all together and mold the sides and edges. We will make them in a way that will use less firewood, plus we will make a chimney out of old cans. This will keep the smoke out of my eyes."

Chico picked up a shovel and the bucket. Rafael was outside with a bucket and shovel also.

"Let's go together," Rafael suggested. "Old Mr. Acosta has some horses and cows up the hillside over that way," he said, pointing. The two boys took off for outside of town.

Chico knew that the women needed to mix the horse manure with sand, straw, and mud.

The boys didn't take long to find horse manure. They began to fill their buckets under the watchful eyes of Mr. Acosta's cows. It wasn't the most pleasant smell, but it wasn't too bad.

All of the sudden a big *guatuza* (gwa-TOO-sah) the size of a big rabbit crawled out from under some bushes. Chico grabbed Rafael's arm and pointed. At first the animal didn't see the boys; his little pointed nose sniffed the air as if smelling the boys' scent on the wind. The little rounded ears wiggled back and forth as it listened. Instantly the boys dropped their buckets and shovels and took off chasing the creature. It ran through some nearby grass, but its yellow-brown hairs couldn't hide in the green grass. Rafael was gaining on it. It darted to the right. Chico turned with the animal. The poor thing, scared out of its mind, turned left then back to the right. It darted around and ran as fast as its four little legs could go. Rafael took a flying leap and grabbed its short little tail, but it slipped between his fingers. Chico kept up the chase. He wanted this *guatuza*. It would make a good meal. Chico stepped in something sticky but ignored it and continued to run. The *guatuza* turned again and ran down the hillside. Chico was getting close. Leaping forward, he slid on his belly into some slimy stuff on the ground. The *guatuza* suddenly turned and left Chico in the sticky pile. Rafael ran up. The *guatuza* had escaped into its hole.

Chico sniffed, "What was that horrible smell?"

Rafael said, "Ugggggh" and wrinkled up his nose. Chico looked down at his shirt and pants. "What a stink!!!! *Wakala*!!" Chico had cow poop smeared from his face to his chest and on down to his feet. It was everywhere! Fresh cow poop! Rafael sat on the ground and laughed. Chico tried to wipe it off, but it stuck to his hands and to his clothes.

"Stop laughing," commanded Chico. "This is NOT funny."

"This is even funnier than the donkey ride last week."

"Only because it's not you!" declared Chico.

The only way to the creek for a bath was straight through town. Mama was waiting for the bucket of horse manure. What could Chico do? "Please take my bucket to my mama," pleaded Chico.

As they neared the church, Mama looked up and saw the boys. "Chico, Chico," she called. Chico looked the other way. He couldn't go near the group of ladies if he smelled like cow poop.

"Chico," she called again. "Over here right now!" He couldn't ignore his mother. He reluctantly drew closer.

As he and Rafael neared, some of the younger teenage girls came out to meet them and take their buckets. Smelling Chico they stopped abruptly. The girls began snickering at his appearance. Wrinkling their noses and turning their heads, they laughed out loud. The other women, hearing the laughter, walked out to see what was so funny. The group laughter began slowly and built. It was contagious. Rafael began to laugh. Chico felt mortified. He looked up and saw his Mama trying not to laugh. She sputtered and, with wrinkled eyebrows, bit her lip. A smile crept across her face. She covered her mouth and laughed. Everyone was giggling and laughing.

Chico thought, *I must be really funny-looking with this yellow-brown poop smeared all over me. I know I stink!* Chico smiled back at the women. A giggle rose from deep inside. As it made its way up to his mouth, it burst forth as a full laugh. Chico held his head high and strolled by, laughing. He headed straight for the creek.

That evening Mama said, "Chico, José's sister usually helps his mother, but she just had a baby and can't help right now. So Rafael's mother and I made arrangements for you boys to go help José's mother make and sell *rosquillos* (rose-KEY-yos). Do you think you can behave? No donkey rides or *guatuza* chases?"

Chico was nodding his head up and down. She continued, "You will help her make and bake them. Plus, you will take them up to the paved road and sell them. She will pay you something for helping."

"Wow, a real job!" responded Chico.

Early the next morning, Chico was at Mrs. Mendez's house adding wood to the cook fire where corn was boiling. Chico and Rafael helped her take the big pot off the stove. They washed the puffed-up grains of hot corn. Rafael turned the crank as Chico fed the hot corn into the grinder. Corn mush emerged from the grinder. Mrs. Mendez put it on the long table and began to mix it with white cheese and pig fat. With the mixed-up dough the boys began to help make little ring shapes. Chico scraped the burning fire out of the big round mud oven when it had a red glow on the inside. The *rosquillos* were placed on long trays inside the oven to bake. They didn't take long to bake. The oven was red-hot.

The morning went by fast; the boys were kept busy. Soon all the *rosquillos* were packed into little plastic bags and the little plastic bags into big bags.

Mrs. Mendez told the boys, "My sister's husband, Ricardo, will be here in his truck, soon. He will take you to the road. My sister, Maybel, has a big *comedor* (coh-may-DOOR). You can sell these to the trucks and buses that stop by there. Stay off the road; it is dangerous. The buses and trucks go by fast. My sister will give you a place to spend the night. Then you walk back when you have sold all the *rosquillos*. Bring me the money."

"What do we sell the bags for?" asked Rafael.

"One *Lempira* (lehm-PEER-ah) each," she replied. "Maybel knows you are on the way and will look out for you."

On the outside Chico acted as though this was an everyday occurrence, but inside he was jumping up and down with excitement: a truck ride, seeing the paved road, and who knew what else they would see?

Ricardo drove up in a whirl of dust. The wheels of his truck were as big as Chico was. Up on the truck they threw the bags of *rosquillos* and their backpacks containing a change of clothes. The boys climbed up on top of the bags of corn that filled the truck. As they drove by, they waved at their mamas washing clothes in the creek. A whole flock of blue magpies flew by with their loud "Raah", "Raah" sound. The boys bounced along and looked off in the distance. Over the hills they saw the orange-red leaves of the flame trees.

After about an hour the truck arrived at a big, wooden bridge. Ricardo stopped the truck and jumped out.

"Hey, boys," he called, "how about a nice swim before we go on?"

"All right!" they chorused.

The bridge was high up above the water—taller than any tree they had ever jumped out of into a creek. The bank to the water below was steep. Ricardo stripped off his clothes and stood on the bridge rail high about the water. He jumped out and splashed into the crystal clear water below. Both boys stared with big eyes. That was a long way to jump! Stripping down to their underwear, they climbed up on the bridge railing.

Rafael said, "You first!"

The bridge was high up off the water—taller than any tree the boys had jumped out of into a creek.

Chico stood on the edge of the railing and felt his heart beat fast. "Let's go together," he said.

Rafael climbed up, "Okay, on the count of three."

Ricardo was climbing out of the water and on up the steep bank back to the bridge. "Jump!" he yelled.

Together they counted, "One, two, three!" They bent at their knees and then stood back up. They both giggled. Doing this was too far, too scary.

Ricardo, walking up from behind, said, "Go ahead, boys, jump!" He gave them a big push on their bottoms. With arms and legs swinging wildly and mouths screaming, both boys went sailing through the air. The water engulfed their screams.

Rafael popped up, screaming, "Wow, that was more fun than a donkey ride."

Chico hollered back, "Definitely more fun than cow poop."

The boys climbed out and jumped again and again. Finally Ricardo said, "Let's go!"

The water refreshed the boys. They climbed back up to their spot high on top of the truck. A couple of hours later they arrived at the road. Chico just stared. The road wasn't dusty but was a hard gray rock, all smashed together. A big wind blew Chico's hair when a truck or bus went by. He never had seen a truck go that fast. Buses were on the side of the road; people got on and off. Trucks and cars were parked in front of a large, cement building. Dust flew up from the vehicles as they drove and parked on the area in front of the building. No trees or bushes were around; just dust, rocks, and the road.

Ricardo took the boys inside. The building had a large room with about 20 tables, where several people sat eating big plates of food. Each table had a tiny bowl of salt and a big jar full of spicy peppers sitting on a red tablecloth. They walked straight back into a big kitchen.

Ricardo grabbed a big woman from behind, twirled her around, and gave her a big, long kiss right on the mouth! Chico stared; he had never seen such a display in his life. The other workers in the warm kitchen didn't seem to notice. Ricardo let her go and took a crispy, fried tortilla chip from the pile beside her.

"Hello, my love," he said as he stepped back and gave his wife a playful pop on the bottom. The woman playfully slapped at his hand.

"What have we here?" She spun around to face the boys. "Ricardo, take these cuties out front and give them a nice cold cola."

The boys followed Ricardo back where they came from. Sitting at one of the tables they watched Ricardo as he opened the top of a big, white box. He pulled out two bottles of black liquid. Using a metal object on the wall, he popped off the tops.

"Enjoy!" he stalked back into the kitchen.

The bottle was cold as it touched their lips. Chico took a small sip and felt the sweet liquid bubble in his mouth. He wanted to spit the bubbles out, but the door was too far away. He swallowed and felt the bubbles tickle the back of his throat. He chuckled and stared at Rafael. Rafael snickered as he swallowed. Both boys sat there drinking the sweet, cold, black liquid and giggling. He had heard about soda pops, but he finally had tasted one. He felt so grown up.

The boys could hear Ricardo and Maybel talking and laughing. Soon Maybel flew through the door with two saucers and sat them in front of the boys. *Pupusas (puh-POO-sahs),"* she said as she put the plates down. They looked like greasy tortillas. Chico tore his steaming, hot pupusa in half to reveal creamy white cheese; he took a tiny bite and found it very good.

After the whole bottle of soda, Chico had to pee. He didn't remember seeing any bushes outside. People were everywhere. He saw no private place to pee. Rafael motioned to Chico. They entered the kitchen again. Ricardo sat on the end of a big, long table. He swang his long legs and chatted with Maybel. His eyes followed her every move.

"Where is your latrine?" asked Rafael.

"Through that door," responded a pretty young woman as she stirred a big pot.

Out back the boys found a big patio surrounded by rooms. Orange trees and lemon trees grew in the center. Along one wall were a series of doors. The doors didn't go all the way to the top or all the way to the bottom of the door space. They had signs that read "Men" and "Women." Chico opened one of the "men" doors and found a tiny room with a water-dripping pipe emerging from the wall.

A big man with a towel wrapped around his waist said, "Excuse me, boys. I need to take a bath here." He stepped into the tiny room and draped his clothes over the top of the door.

A man with a basket of oranges pointed to a door and said, "There is the latrine." Chico opened the door and saw a white chair thing. It didn't stink like a latrine but smelled like soap. Peering inside he saw clear, clean water in the white bowl.

"I guess we pee in the water," snickered Rafael. So they did!

Next to the kitchen door was a huge, cement box full of water on one side. He saw a scrub board and a woman washing clothes.

"Wash up, boys," she said as she handed them a big, round green ball of soap. Obediently the boys washed up. "My name is Linda," she said. Chico looked at her. She had soft, brown curls around her small face and had large, brown eyes. The name *Linda* means pretty. *She is pretty,* thought Chico.

As they stepped back into the kitchen, Maybel said, "Get your *rosquillos*, boys. The supper crowd will come by soon. Go out front and ask people if they want to buy a bag."

Out front Chico and Rafael went from person to person. They asked if they wanted to buy *rosquillos*. Chico stuffed the *Lempiras* into his shorts pocket. Dark fell. Still the buses and trucks pulled in.

Several hours after dark, the buses and trucks stopped. Maybel called the boys inside and sat big bowls of steaming, hot soup in front of them. She pulled out of the whitebox bottles of orange liquid and handed them the cold bottles. Chico really liked this bubbly, orange-flavored drink more than he did the black drink.

Maybel led the boys to a room at the far back of the patio.

"You can sleep here," she said as she opened the door to a room that had a bed along each side. A tiny space was between the beds. A window was above each bed. The boys quickly went to sleep; they had had a long day.

Before the sun rose, Chico awoke to a strange squawking sound.

He reached over and punched his buddy, whispering, "What is that sound?"

Rafael sat up and listened as he turned his head sideways. "It sounds like some kind of animal." As soon as they had a tiny bit of light, the boys opened the door and looked around the big yard. On the other side of the yard were several cages the boys had not seen the night before. They wandered around the yard and looked at the animals inside the cages. They saw a *gautuza* and a raccoon. A huge, red bird with a long tail was squawking. Then they saw the source of the noise that had awakened them. With its long, red feathers with blue mixed in, it was the most beautiful bird Chico ever had seen. Tied to an orange tree was a tiny, little monkey with a white face. The monkey held out his hand to Chico. Chico shrugged his shoulders and showed the monkey his empty hands. Then he reached into his pocket and pulled out half a *rosquilla*. The little monkey hungrily grabbed it and popped it into his little mouth. On a little stand sat a parrot cheerfully jabbering nonsensical words. Rafael held out his finger. The bird stepped right up on his finger and jabbered at Rafael. The green bird bobbed his head back and forth. This place was a nature wonderland.

Linda called to them, "Boys, here is the soap and a towel. Get your showers. Afterward go to the kitchen. Maybel has breakfast for you." She laid the items on the ledge beside the back door.

As he bathed Rafael deposited the bird on the top of the shower door. The bird flew in to the shower and perched on Chico's head as the water splattered about. The laughing boys wondered if the bird needed soap for its bath. Rafael offered the bird his finger. He hopped off Chico's head to Rafael's finger.

Cleaned up and ready for the day the boys headed back to the kitchen. Maybel sat plates of *casamiento* (ca-sa-me-IN-toe) at a small table in the kitchen. *Casamiento* means marriage, since the beans and rice are mixed up together.

The green parrot sat on Rafael's shoulder as Rafael ate.

"Looks like you have a new friend," said Maybel as she sailed by with a big smile. "His name is Peanut, because he likes peanuts." She handed Chico three peanuts. Chico handed the parrot the first peanut. Peanut took it with one of his feet and began eating it while he held the peanut to his beak.

The boys started selling *rosquillos* again, with Peanut perched on Rafael's shoulder. After a while the parrot flew over to Chico's shoulder. Late in the morning the weather got really cloudy. About lunch time a driving rain and a good wind began. By late afternoon water was everywhere. The boys had sold all of their *rosquillos*. They spent the rest of the evening helping Maybel in the kitchen. The teen-aged girl was named Janet. She taught them how to wash and dry the dishes. Then she showed them how to line the plates of food up their arms so they could help her carry food to the tables. Peanut always was close by.

Rain fell all night. Peanut sat on the edge of the window with his head tucked under his wing. In the morning Chico was worried. *What if the rain continues? We can't walk home in pouring rain.*

Maybel cheerfully said, "Looks like I have helpers for another day!" For a place that had so many people cooking, cleaning, and working, Maybel could find more tasks for the boys to do.

They worked all morning long. Maybel fed them well. Late in the afternoon, she asked the boys to go to the store-room in the far corner of the yard and bring her some flour.

As the boys entered the room they noticed the big calendars on the wall. They were women's pictures; the woman in the pictures had on NO clothes. Chico and Rafael stared. They never had seen women like these before. In one a woman sat on a big motorcycle. She didn't have on any clothes except tall red shoes! Chico felt that quivering feeling in his stomach again.

"We shouldn't look. It's a sin," stated Rafael, as he looked for the flour. Chico just stood there and stared at the woman.

Rafael lifted up a big sack. "Come on help me, Chico, and get the other sack."

Chico picked up the sack but didn't take his eyes off the woman on the motorcycle as they backed out of the store-room. Back in the warm kitchen Janet smiled at Chico as he entered with the flour.

"Put it over here, my love," she sweetly said. Chico suddenly felt his face turn red. He knew that looking at the naked girl was wrong. He quickly moved out to the front room. He opened the big, white box and stuck his head inside to cool his face off.

That night as they lay in bed, Chico asked Rafael, "Do you ever get a shaky feeling in your stomach?"

"Yeah, after eating bad beans," laughed Rafael.

"No, silly, I mean like at church or when we saw the calendar of the naked woman."

"Yeah, that is God's Spirit telling me something."

"Do you mean, it was God's Spirit telling me that I shouldn't look at the calendar?"

"I told you not to look. It was a sin."

"My papa says that men don't need God."

Peanut jabbered on the window sill and bobbed his head up and down.

"Well, God was talking to you today, even if you think you don't need him," responded Rafael.

"Do you think the rain will stop soon?" Chico said as he changed the subject. He was feeling uncomfortable with this conversation.

"Hey, you can change the subject, but God is trying to tell you something. Someday you better listen." Chico turned on his side and listened to the rain pound down on the tin roof.

Road sign to Reitoca.

NINE

Mama Gets Sick

*

Chico didn't want to talk about God any more, so he turned over and tried to sleep. The rain poured down all night. Typical for Chico, his thoughts kept him worrying most of the night.

Rain also fell most of the day. Chico and Rafael kept busy working for Maybel. Chico managed to avoid going to the storeroom until Friday afternoon. Maybel asked him to bring her a bag of sugar.

Chico heard noises emerging from the storeroom. He entered slowly and saw Janet. She was kissing the man that Chico had seen with the basket of oranges. They were kissing and didn't even see Chico enter. Chico cleared his throat.

"Hey, cutie," she said looking up. "What do you need?"

"Sugar," replied Chico. Not wanting to look at the girl or the man, his eyes darted around the room and again found the picture of the naked woman on the motorcycle. That sick, trembling feeling crept up from his stomach to his throat. He forced his eyes down to the floor as he felt the heat and red color run up to his face.

"Here, sweetie," the girl said as she handed him the sugar. "Don't be all embarrassed. Don't tell Miss Maybel what you saw. Okay?" Chico heard her say as he backed out of the storeroom.

If this was God speaking, he sure chose a funny way, Chico muttered to himself. *Why doesn't he just talk to me the way Rafael does instead of talking to my stomach?*

Saturday arrived. The rains finally had stopped. The boys wanted to start walking home early. Maybel told them, "Take the path. It will lead to the bridge. On the other side of the bridge to the right, you will find another path. The path is quicker for walking than the road is."

The boys said their good-byes to everyone and especially to Peanut. "Thanks for not telling," said Janet as she hugged Chico good-bye.

Rafael walked the path and sang a song, "Be careful, little hands, what you do. Be careful, little hands, what you do. God the Father up above is looking down in love." Then he switched to, "Be careful, little feet, where you go. Be careful, little feet, where you go. God the Father up above is looking down in love." Then Rafael started a verse about being careful where you look. Chico remembered Janet and the man in the storeroom. He remembered the calendar; he knew that God the Father is up above looking down.

The path suddenly ended at the river. *Where is the bridge? Nothing is left but the posts.* It looked all wrong. The banks of the river were washed clean. The river was still muddy and brown. Looking down the river they saw twisted and broken pieces of what once was a bridge. The rains had taken out the bridge. How could they cross?

Rafael, with wide eyes, said, "Let's walk down a way and see if the river spreads out and gets shallow."

112

Chico shook his head up and down, and thought, *How will we ever cross this river! I don't want to spend the night out here!*

They walked along through brush and tall grass. They started down a steep hillside. A little, green snake slithered across in front of Chico and startled him. Chico lost his footing and slid a short distance in the mud.

"Careful!" he told Rafael. About that time Rafael lost his footing. Down he went sliding in the mud. Rafael hollered. Chico turned to look at Rafael. Rafael grabbed at the grass on the side of the hill, but it pulled out in his hands. He grabbed at Chico's legs. Chico fell. They both screamed. They slid for a few feet, before they could get a grip hold. Muddy but unhurt, they laughed and continued working their way down the steep hillside. Finally they arrived at a wide place in the river. The wide place made the water much more shallow. The water was moving quickly, but it looked to be only about waist high.

Stuffing their *Lempiras* deep into their pockets, Rafael stepped into the water. He had difficulty walking because of the swiftly moving waters. At one point the water was up chest high. Rafael slipped and grabbed Chico, who slipped. The water began to take both boys down stream.

"Swim!" shouted Rafael.

Chico didn't need to be told. He was swimming. Slowly and way down stream the boys finally reached the edge. Climbing out, they sat down on the shore. Chico reached into his pocket. Yes! He still had the money. Rafael quickly checked his pockets. He also still had his money. They sat there catching their breaths.

"Let's get moving," said Chico. "We have a way to go before dark. We have to climb the hill we slid down." Chico didn't want to spend the night on the trail. He had done that once on the way to Porvenir.

They climbed the hill and reached the spot where the bridge should have been. The sun was straight up overhead and blazing down on them. Chico wished he had one of the cold, bubbly drinks from the white box.

The boys followed the path and arrived in Reitoca as the sun was setting. Mama was glad to see Chico. "We were worrying about you, but I knew that Ricardo and Maybel wouldn't let you leave until the storm passed over. Run over and give Mrs. Mendez your money. Then I'll have some supper ready for you," Mama said.

Mrs. Mendez took the money, counted it out, and then handed Chico and Rafael 15 *Lempiras* each. "Give this to your Mama," she said.

Chico ran home and proudly handed the money to Mama. "Oh, Chico, I'm so proud of you—a real man bringing home money!" she said as she hugged him. Chico fell asleep that night as he proudly thought, *Mama said I was a real man.*

The next morning, Chico told Rosa about the slipping and sliding on the trail. Papa walked through the room and said, "A real man works in the fields, not doing women's work baking. Next week you will help me get the field ready to plant corn."

For the next several weeks Chico worked with Papa as Papa cleared the fields. It was a tedious task and rather boring after Chico had been at Maybel's place for a week. Fortunately, Papa didn't say much; Chico didn't either, so they didn't get into any arguments.

One day as Chico and his papa, returning from the fields, got closer to their adobe house, they heard baby Lupe crying.

Entering the house they knew something was wrong. Rosa was holding the crying baby on her hip as she stirred a pot of beans cooking over the wood-burning stove.

"Where is your mother?" asked Papa in a concerned voice. Rosa motioned toward the other room of the little house. Almost running Papa and Chico entered the front room. Lying in bed was Chico's mother. Chico never could remember seeing his mother in bed during the daytime. As Papa tenderly touched her cheek, she opened her eyes and moaned, "I'm sick." Papa responded, "You are burning with fever." Mama whispered, "So is the baby."

Chico took the feverish baby from Rosa and walked around outside until the baby calmed down and quit crying. *He is such a sweet little fellow*, thought Chico sadly.

Papa came out to the house and raked his hand through his hair. As he took the sleeping baby out of Chico arms, he slowly spoke, "Chico, run over to your grandmother's and your aunt's. See if anyone has any medicines."

Chico ran off to see his grandmother. Chico's grandmother gave him a big hug. Chico blurted out that his Mama and baby brother were bad sick with fever.

"Do you have any good medicine that would help?" asked Chico. Shaking her head slowly she replied, "No, no, but you should take her to the *curandero*." Chico's eyes got huge; the *curandero* used herbs and prayers to the spirits. He was kind of scary.

Chico said, "Okay, I'll tell my papa, but first I'm going to run over to Aunt Aura's and see if she has any good medicine." Chico took off running as he hollered over his shoulder, "Bye, Grandma."

Chico's Aunt Aura was outside her little house hanging her freshly washed clothes on the fence around her house. "Hello, Chico," she called out as he got closer. "How is your family?" she asked.

"That is why I'm here," Chico replied. "My mama and baby brother both have a fever. Do you have any good medicine for fever?"

"Oh, Chico, I'm so sorry, but two days ago one of your cousins had a fever. I used the last pill. Did you ask Grandmother?"

"Yes, I was just there. She doesn't have any pills, but she told me that we should take them to the *curandero*," informed Chico.

"Hmmm. I don't know about that," said Aunt Aura. "The *curandero* prays to the spirits. Since your mama is a Christian now, we shouldn't seek healing from the spirits but from the Lord. The Bible tells us not to seek out the spirits, or they will harm us. As Christians we pray only to God."

Aunt Aura put her hand on Chico's shoulder, looked him in his big, brown eyes, and said, "Trust Jesus. I will pray for your mama and baby brother." Chico suddenly noticed again the trembling, quivering feeling in his stomach. It didn't start with the worry over Mama and Baby Lupe. It started with her words, "Trust Jesus."

"Thank you, Aunt Aura. I'll tell Papa what you said." Off ran Chico.

When he arrived back at home, his papa was waiting. Chico quickly explained that no one had any medicine. "But Grandma thinks we should take them to see the *curandero*."

"I don't know," Papa said thoughtfully and slowly. "They both are very sick." Chico replied, "But Aunt Aura says the Bible tells us not to seek the help of the spirits— that we should trust God and pray only to Him."

"Humph," Papa said. Their little town of Reitoca had no health center, no doctor, no nurse—no one to help them.

The next morning Mama didn't get up to fix breakfast. Rosa was up fixing sweet coffee, tortillas, and refried beans. Chico tried to help Rosa care for their other brothers and sisters. Thank goodness no one else in the family was sick. Rosa made sweet rice water. Chico carefully dripped it into the baby's mouth. Chico carried and chopped firewood. He went to the river and carried back big buckets of water. He helped Rosa clean. He and Rosa had a difficult time getting all the work done that Mama did every day.

The next day Papa paced back and forth across their little house. He rubbed his hands through his hair. Finally he said, "Chico, you take care of things. I'm going to walk over the hill to Alubarin and see if the little store there has any medicine for fevers or if the man that owns a truck will take your mama into the city to the hospital."

Late that afternoon Papa returned. He walked slowly with his head down. "No medicines are left in Alubarin. The man's truck is broken down," he said sadly.

That night as Chico laid down on his little straw mat to sleep, he heard his Papa say, "Oh, God, please send us help. Please God, don't let my wife and baby die. Please send us help. Only you, God, can help us. You are our only hope."

Papa praying? Mama must be about to die! cried Chico to himself. He knew that help couldn't get to them. The bridge was gone. The only way into the community was a long way around and crossing through the river. Chico lay his head down and worried what they would do if Mother or the baby died. He didn't even want to think about it. A lump formed in Chico's throat as he tried to stop the tears from flowing. If Papa was praying, things really must be serious.

Early the next morning Chico sat rocking the baby when the green Jeep drove by kicking up lots of dust. Chico's heart leaped up. *Help is here!* Chico wanted to run down the road to the little church where the Jeep had stopped, but the baby had just gone to sleep. The poor little fellow felt so hot in Chico's arm.

A few minutes later Rafael ran up and hollered, "Chico! Run quick. The man in the green Jeep brought his wife, a nurse, and lots of medicine! Bring your mother and baby brother to the little church. The wife of the man in the green Jeep will give them medicine!"

The green Jeep arrives with a trailer and tractor behind it.

Chico handed the baby to his sister, Rosa, and ran inside to find his papa. Papa, sitting on the side of the bed, motioned for Chico to be quiet. Mama lay so still. Chico stopped at the door, "Papa?" he quietly said. Papa sadly looked up. Chico quietly told Papa the joyous news. Mama opened her eyes. In a very quiet voice she said, "Take the baby, Chico. I'm too sick. I can't walk that far." Papa nodded his head at Chico as if to say, "Hurry."

Chico took the baby from Rosa and hurried down the road. A line of people stood outside the little church. Noticing the man in the green Jeep, Chico walked straight to him and held out his little brother. The man took the baby inside to the woman from the green Jeep. Chico followed. The nurse took little Lupe and carefully began checking over the baby. She put a small tube in each of her ears and put a little flat thing on the baby's chest. She injected the baby with medicine. She prepared some pink medicine and asked Chico, "Is anyone else in your family sick?" Chico explained that his mama was so sick that she couldn't walk to the church for care. The lady in the green Jeep kindly replied, "I will be at your house in just a few minutes. You can show me the way."

Chico sat and watched all his neighbors waiting in line to see the woman in the green Jeep. As he watched, Chico remembered his papa's prayer from last night.

The woman and man in the green Jeep quickly followed Chico home. The woman sat down on the edge of the bed beside his mother. She touched Mama's forehead and used the tubes to listen to her. Then she gave his mother two shots. She asked Rosa to bring some rags and a bucket of cool water. She lovingly began to put the cool rags on Mama. She changed the cool cloths every few minutes. The man in the green Jeep placed his hands on Mama's shoulders and prayed for God to heal Mama. The nurse fixed a special drink for Mama and told Rosa to make sure Mama drank a little every few minutes. After a little while Mama looked up at Chico and smiled. The woman prayed and asked God to heal Mama. Chico just knew that his mama would get better now.

As the woman in the green Jeep started walking back to the little church, Chico ran up to her and said, "Thank you for healing my mama. Last night my papa prayed that someone would heal my mama."

"Thank you," replied the woman, "but I didn't heal your mama. God did! I just helped. God used me to help your mother, but God is the one who heals." The woman continued, "Just as God created and made us, He uses that same power to heal our sick bodies. Sometimes He uses other people's knowledge to help. But God is the one who heals."

That afternoon Chico told his father what the woman from the green Jeep had said. Papa paused and then slowly said, "I guess if God is in control of everything, and if God has all power, then He has to be the one that heals us." A big smile broke out on Papa's face. Chico stared at Papa. *What a strange thing for Papa to say!* he thought.

That evening Papa said, "Rosa, will you take care of Mama and Baby Lupe? I want to go to the church meeting."

Rosa and Chico stared at Papa. Finally Rosa said, "Sure."

Papa added, "I want you to go with me, Chico."

That night Chico stood outside the window where he and Papa always stood. Papa said, "I think we need to go inside and sit down." Bewildered, Chico didn't say a word.

Chico sang some of the songs he knew, while Papa just stood there, not singing. Papa looked like he really was listening when the man from the green Jeep spoke.

"When we heard that the bridge into Reitoca had been washed out, we knew that you would need help," the man said. "But fortunately we knew of another way into Reitoca. We had to cross the river. It is a long and difficult way." He continued, "But we have only one Way to God. Jesus is the only Way. He is the bridge to God. We cannot reach God by being strong or by being good—only through Jesus."

Papa leaned forward on the bench and listened intently. When the man asked if anyone wanted to pray and put his or her confidence and faith in Jesus, Papa jumped up and quickly stepped to the front of the church. He knelt down and wiped tears from his eyes. Chico sat on the bench and was too stunned to know what to think. For the second time in two days Papa was praying. What was happening? That quivering feeling was back in Chico's tummy. It seemed to urge him to move.

TEN

The Rabbit Gift

*

Chico stared at his papa's back as Papa prayed. Chico wanted to move and kneel beside Papa, but his legs felt paralyzed. On the walk home Papa smiled the whole way. Chico was too shocked to say a word. Papa was humming! He was happy!

When they arrived home, Mama was sitting up in bed and was eating a bowl of soup. Baby Lupe was sleeping quietly beside her. Papa sat beside Mama and hugged her. "Now, I understand," he said.

Every day Mama got stronger. Every afternoon when Papa returned from the fields, he sat at the table and read Mama's Bible. Well, Mama didn't have a whole Bible—just the New Testament, but she called it her Bible. Papa read some of it every day. Chico thought, *It keeps him busy. He leaves me alone.* Papa had been kinder and easier to live with since he was reading the Bible and praying.

Walking to school one day, Chico met up with José and Rafael. The three boys talked along the way. Suddenly a big, green iguana ran out into the road in front of the boys. Shouting in delight, the boys took off chasing it.

Chico quickly grabbed a handful of small rocks out of the road. Each boy reached into his hip pocket to find his homemade slingshot. No Honduran boy ever would be without his slingshot made from wood and the rubber from an old inner tube. The two-foot-long reptile ran up a tree. The boys took shots at it, but no one got close. The iguana hid in the leaves of the tree. "Come on," hollered Rafael as he began running. "We will be late for school." Chico and José crammed their slingshots back into their hip-pockets. That iguana would have made a delicious meat to go with rice.

Saturday morning the green Jeep arrived as it kicked up the dust from the road. The man in the green Jeep waved at the boys on the side of the road. The boys quickly went into action, as they chased after the Jeep. When the green Jeep was around, the boys knew something fun was about to happen.

The green Jeep stopped by the church. Chico and the boys climbed up on the rack on top of the Jeep so they could see and hear everything. The rack was the boys' front-porch view of everything.

The man from the green Jeep was talking to the men about their crops and how the corn was growing. They talked about the rains and when they could expect to pick the corn. The men talked about how much they needed meat in the town. No one had any cows. They had few chickens. Most chickens had died in the big storm. The people hadn't had meat in a long time.

Chico couldn't remember the last time he had eaten fried chicken. Rafael's little brother said he wanted chicken soup. The boys laughed and playfully punched each other while they talked about their favorite foods.

122

One of the papas told the boys to be quiet. The boys had been laughing and talking so much they missed the end of the meeting. The man in the green Jeep was inviting everyone to the little church that night.

That night at church, the singing was great fun! All the people clapped their hands in time with the music and joyfully sang out loudly about God's love. Then the man from the green Jeep told about God's Son, Jesus, and His love for each person. Chico tried not to listen, because when he listened in church, he always got the strange feeling in his stomach. Rafael's little brother went to sleep and almost fell off the bench. Chico giggled; his mother tapped him on the shoulder. Then Chico pulled out of his pocket a big grasshopper and slipped it into Rafael's little brother's shirt. Soon the little boy was wide awake and jumping around as he pulled at his shirt. The grasshopper jumped out of the shirt and landed on Rosa's dress. She picked it up and threw it out the window. Chico was trying his best to not laugh out loud. Chico's mother grabbed his ear and pulled it really hard.

Chico had to pay attention again. The man in the green Jeep was talking about God's gift to people—a gift of forgiveness that we are to accept. Chico felt that funny feeling again in his tummy. That feeling stayed in his tummy whenever he was at church. Chico knew about Jesus, but he didn't understand what the man from the green Jeep meant when he said, "A gift is no good unless you accept it."

December first arrived. School was out for Christmas holidays. Not that Chico wanted to be in school, but at least it was something to do. Chico not only was bored but was still a little mad at his little sister, Nanci. They had been fighting earlier. Chico couldn't even remember why. When he didn't have anything to do, he always seemed to fight with his sister. She could be so irritating.

Chico took his slingshot out of his back pocket. He picked up a small rock and tried to hit the fence post. Ahh—he missed. Sitting under the tree was his friend, Rafael, and Rafael's little brother. They weren't doing anything, either. With a deep sigh Chico sat down with them and looked up at the sky. No clouds in the pure blue sky and nothing to do. They boys just sat there.

Then the green Jeep suddenly appeared. The rack on top was loaded with rolls of wire mesh. When the Jeep stopped, the boys looked inside. The inside was full of cages with beautiful rabbits! Big, white, furry rabbits! The rabbits were much larger than Chico had ever imagined rabbits being. The boys, squealing with delight, helped the man from the green Jeep unload the rabbits. The man asked the boys to give the rabbits water. They laughed and poked their fingers through the cages. They touched the rabbits' pink noses as they poured water in the clay bowls in each enclosure.

Chico remembered the wild, brown rabbit he had seen on his trip to Porvenir. It was not nearly as large as these rabbits were.

The man from the green Jeep helped all the papas build the wire boxes. As they worked the man from the green Jeep said, "They are easy to take care of. The boys can find plenty of grass and leaves for the rabbits in the woods. Their meat is healthier than beef, pork, or even chicken. Rabbits will have babies every month. They usually have from six to eight bunnies. So you can have rabbit to eat every week."

"They are too cute to eat!" said Rafael.

All the men laughed. Rafael's papa said, "They taste too good to keep as pets." The man from the green Jeep responded, "Don't give them names! You don't name animals that you eat!"

The men chuckled.

124

Chico helped his papa. Bending the wire and forming it into pens was difficult work. The man from the green Jeep reached in and picked up a big, squirming, wiggling, white, fluffy rabbit. He picked it up by the back of the neck just like a mother cat picks up kittens. These rabbits were as big as small dogs. They had paws with sharp claws. The man warned everyone to be careful; the claws could scratch them. Rabbits scratch very deeply. He showed them how to hold the rabbits carefully so they wouldn't get scratched.

The man from the green Jeep held out the rabbit to Chico. Chico was excited but also scared! He didn't want to be scratched. Besides, the rabbit looked heavy and was wiggling his hind legs.

The man from the green Jeep holds a rabbit like the one Chico received.

Chico reached out. The rabbit jumped about. Chico jumped back. Everyone laughed. Chico wanted the rabbit, but he wasn't sure.

The man from the green Jeep said, "Go ahead; reach out and take the rabbit. I am giving you the rabbit as a gift." He said, "You have to reach out and take it."

Chico could feel his heart beating fast and hard. The man waited a moment and then said, "I can't give it to you unless you reach out and take it."

Chico swallowed hard; he waited a moment more.

The man from the green Jeep said, "A gift is no good unless you accept it."

Chico slowly reached out and took the wiggling rabbit. He was very careful to hold the rabbit by its neck and with his other hand to hold the rabbit behind its hind legs. It was heavy but beautiful. A big smile spread across Chico's face. *Papa and I are going to raise rabbits!* he thought. *I will pick green leaves to feed the rabbits. I will give them water. I am so glad I reached out and accepted the rabbit gift.*

Chico carefully put the rabbit in the cage he and his papa had built. He helped his papa carry it home.

* * * * *

That night as Chico lay down on his straw mat to sleep, he thought about all that had happened in the last few days. Then he remembered the church service. Chico knew it displeased God when he fought with his sister or with Calvin. *Looking at the calendar at Maybel's was sin,* he thought. *Pulling pranks on Rafael's little brother wasn't kind.*

Chico remembered when Rafael told him that the funny feeling in his tummy was God trying to talk to Chico. *I need God's forgiveness and love!* he thought. Chico thought about what the man from the green Jeep had said about

126

The people of Reitoca make rabbit cages for the new rabbits
that the man in the green Jeep brought.

having to accept God's love and forgiveness. He said that it
was a gift that you had to reach out and accept, just like the
gift of the rabbit. Since Papa had prayed, he was a changed
man. He didn't yell at Chico; he wasn't as angry. Chico was
sick and tired of the funny, quivery feeling in his tummy.
Maybe he also needed to pray and put his trust in Jesus.
Calvin was a whole new kid. Chico's papa also was
changed. Maybe Chico needed to talk to God and begin to
be a whole new kid also.

Chico knelt down on his straw mat. Everyone in the
house was asleep. He prayed quietly.

"God, please forgive me for the wrong things I have
done. For looking at the calendar, for being mean to my sister and to Rafael's little brother, and for all the other things.

God, I accept your gift of forgiveness and love. I know that you sent Jesus to die for me. I trust you. Amen."

Chico lay down on his straw mat. A big smile spread across his face. The quivering feeling in his tummy was gone. In its place was a good feeling of love and peace. Chico wanted to tell everyone how good he felt. He felt like a whole new kid—all because the man in the green Jeep visited his little town of Reitoca.

People of Reitoca view the new rabbit cages.

APPENDIX

Study Guide
for
The Man in the Green Jeep

*

Here are some ideas to help you present to your students *The Man in the Green Jeep*. Use the study-guide questions in these ways:

• Ask your students to keep a notebook or journal and record their answers to the questions as they progress through the book.
• Use all or some of the questions for a whole-class discussion.
• Divide your students into small groups. Ask them to answer one or two of the questions and present to the class their answers.
• Ask students to work in pairs to write answers to the questions.
• Use some or all of the questions for quizzes, if you are in a learning setting that facilitates this.

• Pull out vocabulary within the reading that you want the students to learn. If you are in a learning setting that facilitates this, make these words part of your spelling unit.

• Depending on the language experience of your class, feel free to omit questions or add some of your own.

Chapter 1: The Storm

1. Discuss Chico's family. What are the names of the family members?
2. Why was Papa worried?
3. Describe the home of Chico and his family.
4. What did the family eat at mealtime?
5. Name four things Chico liked about school.
6. Compare and contrast life in Reitoca before the storm and to life there after the storm. (Make a chart on the board.)
7. Why did Chico need to go for help?
8. Research old Lenca Indians mentioned in this chapter (use the computer and/or library.)
9. Talk about Aunt Sara's family. What were the names of the family members?
10. Discuss family trees. Ask the students to make family trees of their own families.

Chapter 2: Aunt Sara's

1. What is hunger? (Hint: How do you feel when you are hungry?) What is the difference between being hungry and hunger?
2. Describe Chico's condition when he arrived at Aunt Sara's house.

3. How did Marvin help Chico?
4. Why do you think Marvin wanted to help Chico?
5. How did Aunt Sara revive Chico?
6. What did Chico eat for his first meal at Aunt Sara's house?
7. How did Aunt Sara share the Gospel with Chico?
8. What did Marvin and Chico talk about when they were in the tree?
9. What did Marvin tell Chico about his throat/heart?
10. Describe the church service and Chico's concerns for his family during the prayer.

Chapter 3: Help Arrives

1. Describe the activity by the creek.
2. Describe Chico's walk back to Reitoca.
3. Make a time line of events from the time when Chico went to Porvenir to when he returned to Reitoca.
4. Play shadow tag as Chico and Marvin did in this chapter.
5. How does Marvin know Jesus entered his heart?
6. What did Chico tell his family about his trip?
7. What did Chico tell his friends about his trip?
8. Why did the man in the green Jeep help the people in Chico's village?
9. How did life begin to change in Reitoca after the man in the green Jeep visited?
10. Who was Don Felix?
11. Why do boys and girls carry water differently?
12. Why did Papa begin to worry again?

Chapter 4: The Well

1. Why did the people of Reitoca need the well?
2. How was the community able to dig a new well?
3. How did people in the community help each other with the new church building?
4. What did people in the community need to complete the church? How long did they wait?
5. Describe the making of adobe bricks. (Try this with your class.)
6. What does "under conviction" mean? How was Chico "under conviction" after the dump-truck incident?
7. What kind of person was Calvin?

Chapter 5: The Fight

1. Why did Chico and Calvin fight? How was each boy injured?
2. What steps did Miss Alvarez take to solve the problem?
3. How did Mama dress Chico's wounds?
4. When do people cry? (Make a list on the board. Possible answers might be, *When they are tired; When they are scared; When they are embarrassed*) Name three reasons that Chico cried.
5. Why did Chico feel dirty and messed up "inside and out"?
6. What did Papa decide Chico should do? Why?
7. Who was Raymond? Describe the relationship between Raymond and Chico.
8. How do you think Chico felt when Raymond gave him the cap?
9. What impact did the instant-camera picture have on Chico's family?

10. Draw a picture of what you think the photo of Raymond and Chico looked like.

11. Why did Chema pour water over the wood he left at Virginia's house?

Chapter 6: The Wedding

1. What wedding preparations did Chema and Virginia make?

2. What wedding preparations did their families and friends make?

3. What sermon did the man in the green Jeep preach?

4. How did Chico feel about the baptism?

5. Where were the people baptized?

6. Describe the wedding service.

7. Describe the baptism service.

Chapter 7: Rosa's Trees

1. What was Papa's reaction to salvation and baptism?

2. Why was Chico allowed to go back to school?

3. Why did Rafael take the "strikes" that Chico should have had? (What Bible story does this bring to mind?)

4. What happened to Rosa's ankle?

5. How was Chico impacted by Rosa's injured ankle?

6. What was the Lucerne tree project?

7. What exciting event happened after the argument between Papa and Mama?

8. What happened at the church the night Papa and Chico attended?

9. Why did Calvin return Chico's cap?

10. Summarize Calvin's testimony.

Chapter 8: The Paved Road

1. Describe the workday at school.
2. Why did Mama need a bucket of horse manure?
3. What is a *guatuza*? Why did Chico want to catch it?
4. Why did Chico and Rafael sell *rosquillos*?
5. Write the recipe for *rosquillos*.
6. What did Janet teach Rafael and Chico to do in Maybel's kitchen?
7. What caused the shaky feeling in Chico's stomach? When had he experienced this feeling before?
8. What did Rafael say caused this shaky feeling?
9. What does the Bible teach us in this situation?

Chapter 9: Mama Gets Sick

1. Describe the journey home for Chico and Rafael.
2. What is the significance of the words that Rafael sang about being careful where you look?
3. Describe Chico's feeling of accomplishment when he gave his mom the money. Make a list on the board of similar experiences that members of the class have had in feeling good about having accomplished something. (The teacher may lead off by giving some of her own!)
4. What happened to Mama and the baby? What illness/condition do you think they had?
5. What advice did Grandmother give Chico?
6. What advice did Aunt Margarita give Chico?
7. What did Papa do?
8. How did God answer Papa's prayers?
9. What did the nurse tell Chico when he thanked her?
10. What happened at church that night?

Chapter 10: Rabbits

1. What did Papa read as Mama and baby Lupe recovered from their fever?
2. What gift did the man in the green Jeep give to Chico?
3. How did he use the rabbit as a means for witnessing?
4. What happened to Chico as he lay in bed thinking about his new gift?
5. Write Chico's prayer.
6. Make a list of the ways the man in the green Jeep, Raymond, Rafael, Marvin, Calvin, Aunt Sara, and Mama continued to encourage Chico to love Jesus and to know Him as his personal Savior. What lesson do we learn from their examples about loving a lost friend or relative?
7. How can you be a friend to someone who does not know Jesus?

Project Ideas for the Man in the Green Jeep

As your students progress through *The Man in the Green Jeep*, the story lends itself to some interesting projects. Sufficient ideas appear here for each student to find something of interest. If you are in the kind of learning setting that lends itself to this, you can make the project a major test grade. As leader you may think of other ideas.

I. Draw and label a relief map of Honduras.
  1. Include the mountains, rivers, and major cities.
  2. Be sure to include the locations the book mentions.
  3. Show borders to neighboring countries and major bodies of water.
  4. Label everything on the map. You may want to make a map key which would, for example, indicate that you used solid lines for roads and dotted lines for paths.

II. Make a sketch or paint a portrait of the man in the green Jeep. (Refer to page 40 for details.)

III. Make a diorama for one of the following:

Honduran Village
The Wedding
Chico's School
Men Working at the Well
Laundry Day
The Journey from Reitoca to Porvenir
Meeting at the Big Tree

IV. Discuss the significance of

1. The garlic string
2. The big tree
3. Taking firewood to Virginia
4. Missionaries and work teams
5. Carrying buckets

V. At least 15 times people shared the Gospel message with Chico. Discuss in detail four of them. (Below are some suggestions and the page numbers on which the testimony or sharing occurs.)

1. Aunt Sara (p. 29)
2. Marvin talks with Chico about his heart (p. 30)
3. Marvin's testimony (p. 31)
4. Man in the green Jeep delivers shovels, hoes, and wheelbarrows (p. 41)
5. The people give thanks for the new well (p. 50)
6. Forgiveness after the truck incident (p. 56)
7. Team from U.S. (p. 69)
8. Jesus film presentation (p. 70)
9. Wedding sermon (p. 80-81)
10. Rafael's strikes (p. 88)
11. Calvin's testimony (p. 97)
12. "Shaky" feeling in stomach (p. 109)
13. Aunt Aura (p. 116)
14. Nurse's visit (p. 119)
15. Gift of the rabbit (p. 127)

VI. Make a picture book of *The Man in the Green Jeep*. Decide on eight events in the book that you could draw. Write a caption under your picture. (Here are a few examples to consider. You can use these and others you want to include.)

1. The big storm
2. Chico and Marvin in Porvenir
3. Meeting under the big tree
4. Chema and Virginia's wedding
5. Digging a well
6. Going to church
7. Chico and Calvin working together
8. The rabbit gift
9. Rosa's trees
10. Chico prays the sinner's prayer

VIII. From Chico's point of view write journal entries for each of the following:

1. The big storm
2. Trip from Reitoca to Porvenir (Be sure to include plants and wildlife.)
3. Church meeting at Don Felix's house
4. Digging the well
5. Planting beans with Papa
6. The Lucerne tree project
7. A day at school
8. Chico's experiences of realizing that he needed Jesus in his heart

IX. Make a story map. Here is an example of what your story map might include: In the middle of a page or a poster board, write the name of the book and include a picture that represents the story—in this case, the green Jeep.

Divide the paper or poster board into four parts. In the upper left quadrant list the names of the characters. In the upper right quadrant write a description of the setting. In the lower left quadrant list the main events. In the lower right quadrant list the resolution of conflict(s).

X. Describe the chores of the Honduran children.

XI. On the following page is a Spanish vocabulary worksheet (How Much Spanish Did You Learn While You Read *The Man in the Green Jeep?*) After the students complete the book, give them the Spanish worksheet to work individually or in pairs to see how much Spanish they learned. If you, as leader, do not speak Spanish, enlist for help on the pronunciation another person (possibly another teacher) who speaks Spanish. Correct answers to the worksheet exercise are: *1. e; 2. a; 3. i; 4. k; 5. l; 6. m; 7. c; 8. d; 9. g; 10. h; 11. n; 12. f; 13. o; 14. j; 15. p; 16. b.*

How Much Spanish Did You Learn While You Read *The Man in the Green Jeep*?

Match the Spanish word in **Column A** with the definition in **Column B**.

Column A	**Column B**
1. _____ *Cacique*	a. mountains where Chico and his family lived
2. _____ Lapaterique	b. name of Chico's village
3. _____ Lucerne tree	c. name of Aunt Sara's village
4. _____ *rosquillos*	d. gourd-like bowl for scooping
5. _____ *comedor*	e. leader in Honduran village
6. _____ *Lempira*	f. herb used to reduce swelling
7. _____ Porvenir	g. big, fat guitar
8. _____ *jacal*	h. person sick villagers visited
	i. fast-growing tree
9. _____ *guittarón*	j. large rodent the size of a rabbit
10. _____ *curandero*	k. type of cracker made from corn mush, white cheese, and pig fat
11. _____ *pupusas*	
12. _____ *azotecaballo*	l. a type of restaurant
13. _____ *casamiento*	m. money in Honduras
14. _____ *guatuza*	n. hot tortilla filled with white, creamy cheese
15. _____ tortilla	o. means *marriage*—rice and beans
16. _____ Reitoca	p. a flat bread

Order more copies of
The Man
in the Green Jeep
Call toll free: 1-800-747-0738
Visit: www.hannibalbooks.com
Email: hannibalbooks@earthlink.net
FAX: 1-888-252-3022
Mail copy of form below to:
Hannibal Books
P.O. Box 461592
Garland, Texas 75046

Number of copies desired   _____

Multiply number of copies by $9.95   _____

Please add $3 for postage and handling for first book and add 50-cents for each additional book in the order.

Shipping and handling$_____

Texas residents add 8.25% ($1.07) sales tax $_____

Total order $_____

Mark method of payment:

check enclosed _____

Credit card# _____

exp. date_____ (Visa, MasterCard, Discover, American Express accepted)

Name _____

Address _____

City State, Zip _____

Phone _____ FAX _____

Email _____

You'll also enjoy these missions books

The Jungle series, also known as the Rani Adventure Series by Ron Snell. With hilarity, warmth, and spine-tingling suspense, "the Rani Series" trilogy takes readers into the cross-cultural upbringing of Ron Snell, who, with his family, sets aside American comforts to bring the good news of Christ to people in darkness in the Amazon jungles of Peru.

It's a Jungle Out There (Book 1) _____ **Copies at $7.95 =** _____
Life is a Jungle (Book 2) _____ **Copies at $7.95 =** _____
Jungle Calls (Book 3) _____ **Copies at $7.95 =** _____

Rescue by Jean Phillips. American missionaries Jean Phillips and husband, Gene, lived through some of the most harrowing moments in African history of the last half century. Abducted and threatened with death, Jean and Gene draw on God's lessons of a lifetime.
_____**Copies at $12.95=**_____

Beyond Surrender by Barbara J. Singerman. A dramatic story of one family's quest to bring light to a dark and desperate world. The Singerman family serves in Benin, West Africa. They confront spiritual warfare beyond anything they expect when they surrender to missions.
_____**Copies at $12.95=**_____

Add $3.00 shipping for first book, plus 50-cents for each additional book.
Shipping & Handling _____
Texas residents add 8.25% sales tax _____
TOTAL ENCLOSED_____

check _____ or credit card # _____ exp. date_____
(Visa, MasterCard, Discover, American Express accepted)

Name _____

Address _____ Phone _____

City _____ State _____ Zip _____

For postal address, phone number, fax number, email address and other ways to order from Hannibal Books, see page 141